Dev

Devour

Shelly Crane

Editing services provided by Jennifer Nunez

Cover models for the series: Veronica Herwarth and Charlie Heimbach

This book and others from this author are available in Kindle, Nook and Paperback versions in November 2011 through Amazon, Create Space and Barnes & Noble.

Further information can be found at the author's website.

www.shellycrane.blogspot.com

ISBN-13: **978-1466474024**
ISBN-10: **1466474025**

~

This book is dedicated to the people who have recently come into my life in a whirlwind of positive words and encouragement through many avenues. I'll be forever grateful for all the help I received from so many as I wrote this book and others. Through moving, sickness, disappointments and awesome days, you were there and I say thank you!

~

"But often, in the world's most crowded streets,
But often, in the din of strife,
There rises an unspeakable desire
After the knowledge of our buried life,
A thirst to spend our fire and restless force
In tracking out our true, original course;
A longing to inquire
Into the mystery of this heart which beats
So wild, so deep in us, to know
Whence our lives come and where they go.
And many a man in his own breast then delves,
But deep enough, alas, none ever mines!
And we have been on many thousand lines,
And we have shown, on each, spirit and power,
But hardly have we, for one little hour,
Been on our own line, have we been ourselves;
Hardly had skill to utter one of all
The nameless feelings that course through our breast,
But they course on for ever unexpress'd.
And long we try in vain to speak and act
Our hidden self, and what we say and do
Is eloquent, is well—but 'tis not true!"

~The Buried Life by Matthew Arnold~

~

One

There's a game you play. The one where you guess what the shapes and objects the clouds have made above you. Today there was a lady with a long witchy nose, a rabbit, a sailboat. Everyone's perception is different; we all see different things. I personally think you see what you want to see.

I was solely entranced in my gazing. The sun was bright behind me as I lay in the grass, my head on my jacket. My insanely dark black hair was long and almost too warm as it fanned around my head and caught the sunlight. The small hill on the edge of the park was the perfect spying spot. Spying on clouds, on people, on squirrels, but I was alone. Alone here and alone in life. My family used to come here together, but no more. My sister was gone, joined the Navy and would be gone for four years. She couldn't handle the fact that our parents died and decided to fulfill my dad's wish for us to be in the armed forces.

The burglary, and the burglar who took their lives, was something we all wished to forget. Even the Montana police hastened the investigation because things like that just didn't happen in our town. But there I was, stuck in my last year of high school, living with my Pastor's family as a temporary custody home until I graduated and went off to college. I was as alone as I could be.

The sun so bright behind me made the shadow that was suddenly loomed over me startling.

Devour - Shelly Crane

I looked up to see a guy standing by my head looking down at me. He had a little smile, almost wistful, on his lips as he cocked his head to the side. I sat up and twisted to see him better. His eyes were a freakishly bright violet. I'd never seen a guy with purple eyes – well, I'd never seen anyone with purple eyes. It was a rare thing, I guess, but now looking at them like that, they almost seemed natural.

He was wearing a deep green button up shirt with the sleeves rolled up and jeans with a small tear in the knee. Aviator sunglasses hung from his collar. His hair was as black as mine and close cropped. His hands were in his pockets and he continued to stare at me until I spoke.

"Hi."

"Hello, there," he finally said, his voice deep and lilting with a small accent that I couldn't place.

"Can I...help you with something?" I asked since he continued to gaze at me unabashedly.

"Nope. Just enjoying the view," he said and then smiled slightly as he turned to look up at the clouds and then back down to me. "There always seems to be a rabbit and an old lady doesn't there."

"How did you know I was..."

"I guessed. Why else would you be laying here, alone, looking at the clouds?"

I laughed nervously and twisted the ring on my finger; my nervous tick.

"Are you new here? I haven't seen you around. Big Timber is a small town so, you kinda know everyone whether you want to or not."

He laughed and it was delicious and rich making my stomach flip. I frowned. I had a boyfriend. What was wrong with me?

"Yeah, I'm new. Just moved stateside from Zimbabwe. My parents were teachers at one of the schools there. I'm Elijah Thames, but everyone calls me Eli," he said and knelt down in front of me, sticking out his hand in greeting.

"Clara Hopkins."

I took his hand, almost expecting something to happen when our skin met. Though his hand was warm and rugged, it was just a normal handshake.

"Nice to meet you, Clara Hopkins."

"You too, Eli. You came at the perfect time I guess. Second semester starts tomorrow so we all get new classes. It won't just be you getting a new schedule."

"That's nice, I guess. I'm pretty used to being the new kid though."

"Are your parents missionaries or something?"

"Of sorts," he said vaguely and stood. "So, what's there to do in this town on a Sunday afternoon?"

"You're looking at it," I said through a giggle. "This is about it, I'm afraid. There is an old theater in town but it only plays one movie at a time and there's a club here, but I've never been to it. We usually just hang out at the burger place."

"Who's we?"

"What?"

"You said 'we hang out'. Who's we?"

"Oh. My friends and I. My boyfriend," I said and was shocked at how reluctant I was to tell him that.

"Ah, I see. I should have known it wouldn't be that easy, huh?"

"What wouldn't?" I asked though I felt the blush creeping up, knowing exactly what he meant.

He just smiled.

"Well, can I walk you home at least? It'll be getting dark soon."

"Um...sure, I guess." I took the hand he offered and then picked my brown corduroy jacket up, slipping it back on. "So, do you always walk up to strange girls in the park and start conversations?"

"Nah," he said slyly and bumped my shoulder. "They didn't have parks in Zimbabwe."

I burst out laughing and was intrigued by how comfortable we seemed to be together already.

"Where do you live?" I asked him as we hopped onto the sidewalk.

"We bought a place on Buxton."

"The bed and breakfast?"

"Yeah. My parents are all about trying something new."

"Wow. Well, it's a nice house. I've always loved that place."

"It's nice and big. Too big but I guess once you get a house full of guests it won't be big enough. I made my room the basement though, so that should help with the privacy."

"The basement? Won't that be cold and muggy and...creepy?"

"You watch a lot of scary movies, do you?" he said in amusement.

"Maybe I do," I spouted playfully. "I'm sure it's nice enough anyway. But you know, it could be the attic," I said and shivered in mock horror.

"Oh, attic's are *way* creepy."

We laughed and it resounded in the quiet darkening street.

He seemed to know right where he was going so I just walked beside him and let him lead us. Buxton was only a few blocks away from the city park and I lived beside the church near there.

We walked and talked for about a block before trouble turned the corner.

My boyfriend, Tate, was coming down the street in his big 4x4 truck. He was on the wrestling team, the town's pride. He was really good to me, very attentive, and while I enjoyed spending time with him, I wasn't in love with him. And he was a very jealous guy. All he ever talked about was us going to college together next year, but I didn't want to go to college. I wanted to go on a mission trip or maybe apply to a Music or Art school. If my parents were alive, they'd be so disappointed. My dad dreamed of his alma mater and the Army and my mom wanted me to marry right away and find a man to take care of me. Both of those dreams were nil.

But Tate was a sweet guy. Even though he was popular, he was pretty nice to everyone...except guys who tried to talk to me. He once almost pummeled my science lab partner when he stopped me in the hall to get my notes.

Apparently, his mom cheated on his dad all the time and his dad had no inclination to do anything about it. The whole town knew about it but they held a position of status and prime real estate in the town so no one cared, essentially. But Tate had always cared.

"Oh boy," I mumbled.

"What? What's wrong?"

"Nothing's wrong, just my boyfriend. Just don't listen to anything he says for the next five minutes, ok? I'm sorry ahead of time."

"Ok," he said, dragging it out in apprehension.

Tate stopped the truck and I saw it overcome him. His fingers turned white on the steering wheel, his lips grim in a tight line. He opened the door and closed it gently, too gently to be considered normal. It was a façade.

"Hey, Tate. Were you coming to see me?"

"You weren't at home. I was headed to the park to give you a ride…but I see you don't need one what with prince charming walking you home and all," he sneered, glaring daggers at Eli.

"Tate, this is Eli. He's new here and lives near me. We were walking home together, talking about school tomorrow."

"Uhuh."

"Tate," I chided and went to give him a kiss on the cheek. I felt his skin, hot and angry on my lips, before I pulled back. He flicked his eyes to me once before looking back to Eli. "Tate, this is ridiculous," I whispered to him. "Why don't you trust me?"

"It's other guys I don't trust!" he yelled, making me jump. "You have no idea what guys are thinking about."

I took a deep confused breath. He'd never been that vehement before. I glanced over at Eli to apologize, but he looked strange. Almost like he was...in ecstasy. His mouth was slightly open and his eyes hooded as he watched me. His breathing was heavy. I squinted at him and he seemed to snap out of it.

"Come on, man," he said to Tate. "Really, it was nothing. She was just telling me about classes changing and all since I just moved here. She told me she had a boyfriend within the first two minutes of talking to her."

Tate looked at me, his eyes softening a little. I looked at him pleadingly.

He took a hesitant step towards me and when he saw I made no move to step away he caved and pulled me to him.

"I'm sorry, Clara, you know how I get. I can't... It's dumb, I know. I'm really sorry." He pulled back to look at me. "I didn't mean to be like that."

"I know you didn't," I said softly and him being the blonde, beefy guy he was who stood right at my height level, put his forehead to mine.

"How do you even put up with me?" he whispered.

"I don't know," I said jokingly, "you're pretty cute. I guess it makes up for it."

"Pretty cute?" he joked and suddenly dropped to one knee and in his best English white knight accent began to beg. "Oh, please, my darling. My love. Forgive me and my assness!"

This was the Tate I knew and cared about. He was fun, playful and not afraid to make a fool of himself.

I laughed and bowed a little.

"You're forgiven. Now. Tate, this is Eli Thames. Eli, this is Tate Richman. He's captain of our wrestling team and his dad's the mayor," I said proudly.

"Hi," Eli said cautiously and stuck his hand out.

Tate stood and took the hand offered.

"Hey, man. Sorry. I'm can be a bit of an ass when it comes to this girl. I'm sure you can understand," he said with a wry smile.

"Understood." Eli looked back to me and smiled a little sadly. "Well, I guess I'll see you guys tomorrow."

"You can have lunch with us tomorrow," I threw out. "I'm not sure if I'll see you before then, but we eat at the long table right in the middle of the cafeteria."

"Ok. Thanks."

"See ya, man," Tate said and waited for Eli to turn, then pulled me to him, snuggling into my neck. "Oh my gosh, Clara, you smell like something I very much want to eat."

I giggled and pushed him back a little.

"You think you're getting off that easy, buster?"

"What do I owe you this time?" he asked amused and touched his tongue to his lip to think. "Diaper duty? Because if that's it, it was nice knowing you."

"Hey!" I yelled playfully and smacked his chest. "No. Mrs. Ruth has the kids tonight, but you do have to take me home and...watch the last Vampire Diaries I DVRed."

"Ah, Clara," he groaned. "Anything but that."

"Come on, it's not that bad."

"It's torture," he said pointedly and then smiled. "But for you I'd do just about anything."

"I know," I agreed and I did. Tate had reasons to be the way he was and the way he normally treated me would put the Salvatore brothers to shame. But for some reason, I just couldn't move past the feeling that he was just some guy I liked, had feelings for, but knew it wasn't going anywhere. "Come on."

He helped me into the truck and drove the short distance to the Parish. Once we stopped in front of the house, I started to get out but he stopped me.

"Wait. Before we enter the no-touch zone..."

Devour - Shelly Crane

He pulled me to him across the seat and kissed me. Tate was usually a gentleman and knew how far I was willing to let him go. Sometimes he casually tried to push the envelope; he was a guy after all. This was apparently going to be one of those times.

His hand gripped my leg, as if to tug me into his lap. I let him. He seemed fueled by that and as his hands on my hips pulled me closer to him. I heard him groan a little. It rumbled through me and made my heart beat a little faster. I knew it was only torture to do this. I'd never let him do anything more than this. We were both virgins, though I was happier about it than he was. But sometimes, I just needed to feel the glue to the envelope strain a little.

I let him kiss me for a good while, just like that. I ran my fingers through his hair. It'd been a year since we started dating. We'd both always gone to the same school together, always lived in this town. We hung out with the same friends but he'd never seemed interested in me before and I never thought about him that way. I'd been on a few dates with other guys but never really dated anyone exclusively. Then one day, he met me at my locker, alone. It was odd because usually there was a group waiting there for me. As I made my way to him, he smiled bashfully.

"Hey."

"Hey," I had said cheerfully ignorant.

"How was Spanish? I have that next semester."

"Brutal."

"I was afraid of that. So, um...there's this movie playing at the Cineplex, Adam Sandler is in it. Looks pretty good. I was wondering if you wanted to go tonight?"

"Sure. Who else is going?"

"Just you. And me."

"Oh," I had said and even I heard the odd note to my voice. He mistook that as reluctance.

"It's ok if you don't want to go, I just figured it might be fun. It's ok," he had said and started to walk away.

"No, wait. I didn't say I didn't want to go."

"Do you want to?" he'd asked and came to stand closer than he'd ever stood before.

I remembered my pulse had suddenly jumped and I noticed how green his eyes really were for the first time.

"Yeah. I do."

His smile was genuine and a little surprised.

"Great. I'll pick you up at five thirty. We can get something to eat first if you want."

"Yeah. Sure."

He'd walked backwards, grinning, away from me. That night he'd picked me up and we had fun, lots of fun. When he dropped me off I couldn't help but ask why he was all of a sudden interested.

"I can't say it was all of a sudden," he'd answered. "I just wasn't sure if you'd want to and I didn't want things to be weird so I just watched you. But you never looked at me different...so I took a shot." Then he touched my cheek, his thumb sweeping across my cheek bone. "I'm glad I did."

"Me too."

Then he had kissed me and I felt something in me burn, like slow lava. We'd stood there on my parents porch and kissed slowly and gently for a good while before my dad turned the light off and on, making us laugh.

Two months later, when my parents died, he was there for me like no one else. He was the first person to meet me at the hospital waiting room. He held me – just held me – for hours in those uncomfortable chairs as I bawled my eyes out. My sister had been gone on a skiing trip with friends and wasn't there yet. I had been to a movie with my friend who moved to another town, Addison, and found my parents when she dropped me off. Tate stayed with me all night. Took me home, held me as I finally fell asleep on the couch. I don't know what I would have done without him.

And now as he ravished my mouth with skill and restraint I was still thankful for him but, I didn't love him. He had never said the words to me and I wasn't sure what I'd say if he did. I couldn't lie.

"Mmm, Clara, you are driving me every kind of crazy," he spoke huskily against my lips.

"Then maybe we should stop."

"No. No, don't stop," he said and took my lips again.

"Tate," I whispered. "You're not making this easy."

"Then give in to me," he suggested and I could hear the smile in his voice.

"Tate," I chided.

"Ok, ok." He blew a long breath. "It should be illegal for you to look the way you do and me not be able to have you."

"That's so cheesy," I said through a smile.

"I know," he laughed. "Alright, fine. Vampire Diaries in the preacher's house it is."

"Thank you," I said and pressed one last kiss to his lips before climbing out of the truck.

We spent the night like we spent a lot of nights; watching television on my bed, with the door open and a clear view of us from the door. I was allowed to lay by him but there was no kissing in the house. The preacher, Pastor Paul, was very lenient with me but there were certain rules of conduct, especially with Tate, that he was strict about. Despite us being young and all, we were both kind of home bodies. I'd rather sit and watch a movie at home with him than go out with a whole bunch of people. Our friends and I usually had to work pretty hard to get Tate to go out somewhere. He much preferred to be alone with me.

~ ~ ~

I was back, laying in the grass in the park. It all looked so real. The sun was bright and gorgeous behind me as it cast sparkles on the lake. A perfect day. I saw a shadow over me. At first I thought it was Tate but this person was taller and leaner and I felt something coming from him. Like I could feel his interest in me like a tangible thing. He knelt down beside me and I sat up. His face was covered in shadow from the halo of sun around his head. He reached out and touched my face. I gasped at the pleasure his touch elicited from my skin, goose bumps spread widely and I tingled all over. A response I'd never felt before, not even with Tate.

He moved in to kiss me and I was helpless to stop him. His lips almost touched mine. I felt the heat from his breath and a tremor ran through me. I suddenly felt afraid for no apparent reason at all and he moaned, seeming to enjoy my reaction. He pulled me to him and I whimpered as my terror spiked and he continued to hold me to him, like I was something he couldn't live without.

I jolted me eyes open with a start. What was that? I wasn't even asleep yet. Too many vampire shows for me...

The next morning I woke feeling a little strange. The first face I saw was Eli's and I immediately felt guilty. Tate was good to me, though he had his flaws like everyone else. He was very desirable; a hot commodity at our school, and I was lucky he wanted to date me. At least that's what everyone told me. It couldn't be that he was lucky to be with me.

So I threw on my school uniform. Most people hated them, but I loved them for some reason that escaped me. It was a typical uniform; red and black plaid skirt, white collar shirt and a vest that matched the skirt. No knee highs though, thank goodness. We were instructed to wear black ballet flats. After I fixed my hair and threw in some earrings, I made my way downstairs.

After helping Mrs. Ruth with all the babies breakfast - she had five kids under the age of five, the latest being twins who were only four months old - I rushed off to school, a little later than I'd wanted. I came through the gray concrete halls of our prison looking high school looking for Eli. I had wanted to get there before homeroom bell to make sure he found his class easily, but the bell was about to ring. Dang, I was going to be late. The church and the parish were across the street from the school. They shared a parking lot in fact, so I never got a ride with Tate; I didn't need one.

I ran to my new home room just as the last bell rang. I slid into the first empty seat I saw by the door. I noticed Tate across the room, looking at me with amused eyes. He made kiss lips at me as we both turned to face forward.

After the bell rang, we made our way to the hall. I waited for Tate and he studiously threw his arm around my shoulder and kissed my temple.

We walked to my locker and there was Eli. At first I thought he was waiting for me there and wondered what Tate would do, but I saw him reaching into the locker next to mine. He was now my neighbor.

"Hey, Eli," I said.

He looked surprised to see someone knowing his name and almost dropped his books, catching them very cutely in a jumble before they hit the floor and stuffing them in his locker.

"Oh. Hey, guys," he said in that low rumbling voice of his.

"Who do you have for homeroom?"

"Mr. Winepeeno?" he tried and Tate and I both laughed.

"It's Winepegofski. I know, it's an impossible name. I think he's from Russia or Poland or something."

Someone called my name and I looked up to see Ashley. I waved and turned back to Eli.

"A Polish guy teaches U.S. History?" Eli asked with a smirk.

"Welcome to America, Mr. Zimbabwe."

He laughed and leaned on his shoulder against his locker. I looked up to Tate to see him no longer smiling. He was looking between us with a slight frown gracing his brow.

"Tate, who do you have next?" I asked, trying to include him.

"Bishop. Shop," he spouted shortly.

"Ugh, well, we definitely won't share that class. I have Menendez."

"Me too," chimed Eli.

"Huh," Tate said, clearly annoyed. "I'm out. Gonna be late and Bishop will ride me all year."

"Tate," I called and grabbed his arm. "I'll see you at lunch, ok?"

"Ok," he said tightly.

"Hey," I pulled him to look at me and saw a couple freshman giggling at us from across the hall. I ignored them. "I'll miss you," I said to appease him. "It's too bad we don't have anymore classes together."

"Yeah, I'm sure you'll really miss me with Zimbabwe over there," he said low where Eli couldn't hear us.

"I will. He doesn't watch vamp shows with me and follow silly rules at the house I live at. He doesn't know exactly where to find me when he comes to see me and I'm not home. He's just a guy, Tate."

He laughed a small breathy laugh.

"Ok," he conceded. "You better miss me," he joked and poked a finger at my chest gently.

"I already do," I said and accepted his kiss. He usually didn't kiss me on the lips in school, but right then he was letting me have it. I felt his hand on my lower back, pressing me closer. In the distance I heard a whistle from someone and I pulled back to breath. "Wow."

He chuckled.

"I can definitely deal with wow."

"Bye."

"Bye, babe."

I watched him walk away as he bumped fist with someone and they started to jog across the campus.

Then I turned to see Eli still standing there, with a wry look on his handsome face. The fluorescent lights made his hair even blacker. He looked almost ethereal like that. Today he'd worn his hair spiked to the side and I noticed he had his right eyebrow pierced with a small silver rod. I hadn't seen that last night. He was wearing the same jeans as before but with a Queen 1986 Tour shirt. It was his first day, so he didn't have his uniform yet. It always made the new kids stick out like sore thumbs.

"Hey, sorry. I told you he's...I don't know. And I'm sorry about last night too."

"No worries. It's not your fault. So," he grabbed a black messenger bag from his locker and threw it over his shoulder, "can I walk with you to our next class or will I get my spleen removed for it?"

"Ha ha. Yes, walk with me. It's way over on the other side of the gym, so we better get going."

We walked and I saw he was getting quite a lot of attention. I even got the stink eye from a couple of girls and I couldn't help but laugh. He was definitely cute with a bad boy thing going that made me cringe with the cliché of it. He wasn't hot in the traditional sense, I guess. He was a little rugged and jagged, but he was extremely nice and not cocky so that added to his appeal.

"Hi, Clara!" Sarah called as she passed.

"Hey."

"Who's this?" she said and walked backwards beside us to eye him appreciatively.

"This is Eli. He's new."

"Oooh. New meat. I'm Sarah. I'm single by choice, a Pisces, and I'm on the spirit squad with Clara. I'm also free this Saturday."

Eli chuckled and it had the same effect on Sarah as it had on me yesterday. She looked about to jump him right there in the hall, so I saved her some embarrassment.

"Sarah, we're late. You can ogle him at lunch, ok?"

"Ok. Bye, babe! Bye, Eli," she sang his name and flounced away.

"She eats lunch with you?"

"Afraid so. You may as well get used to it now. We hardly ever get new kids at our school and the girls I hang out with are...forward when it comes to guys. You can back out now and I wouldn't blame you."

"No. No, I like a challenge." I looked at him sideways to see him smiling in his profile. "So the spirit squad? I didn't peg you as a cheerleader."

"You pegged right. I'm not," I laughed. "Spirit squad decorates for games and sells tickets and ribbons and stuff. We try to pep people up for events."

"I see. Sounds interesting. And cheerleaders can't do this?"

"Not when they're too busy *getting* busy in the bathroom before the games."

He laughed and I looked at him with a smile. He was so different somehow.

While gazing at him I forgot to watch where I was going and plowed right into a freshman, but he may as well have been Andre' the Giant. He was huge and the fact that I was a girl apparently had no effect on him.

"Watch it," he growled.

"Sorry."

"Why don't you just take your," he slapped my butt hard, "pretty little pampered spirit squad butt back to where you belong and get out of my way."

"Whoa, pal," Eli said and pulled me behind him. I was surprised by it but grateful. "Don't talk to her like that and don't *ever* touch her again."

By this point there was an eager crowd with the word fight dancing in their eyes.

"Who are you, Pippy?" Everyone laughed and snickered. "If I were you I'd watch it. You're not making a very good first impression at this school. First, you're hanging out with spoiled ice queen over here, and now you're messing with me. I'd just go around me and pretend you never got in my way if I were you."

"Sure. I'll do that after you apologize," Eli said calmly.

"I don't apologize to brats who get everything they want. She should apologize for bumping me."

"I did," I mumbled at the same time that Eli said, "She did."

"Whatever-"

"Get to class!" Mr. Brank called from his classroom and everyone scattered. "Now."

"Later, Pippy," the big freshman jerk called. "Later, spoiled brat."

We started to walk and heard the bell. We were still a couple hallways away from class and I saw no point in rushing now.

"Thank you," I said after some time. "I have no idea who he was, but he apparently knows me."

Two

"So, I was just sitting there, minding my own business, when he comes up and asks for my notes from the day before, right in front of everyone. Number one, like I take notes, and number two, like I'd give them to that nerd just because he missed a day for his allergies," sneered Megan, flipping her white, straight as a board blonde hair, making everyone laugh.

Everyone but me and Eli, I noticed.

We'd all piled in as we always did and sat together. Eli had found his way to our lunch table not long after that. He sat across from me and Tate and I introduced him to everyone and the girls swooned appropriately.

Then more stories of their precious existence encounters with the commoners of our high school droned on. Mike tripped a guy and he almost spilled his chili and everyone laughed. Tommy told us how he lifted some band girl's skirt before gym and she'd cried and ran to the office.

As much as I liked my friends, they could be awfully shallow and cruel. Usually Tate wasn't involved in that stuff. He was a nice guy who would talk to anyone but he laughed right along with everyone else on most things.

When it seemed everyone was done with their stories, they started asking Eli questions about where he was from and Megan asked if he was attached to anyone. He answered their questions smoothly and even threw in a joke here and there. He seemed to pass their exam.

Then I saw it; the look and the cold smile directed at me that I'd been waiting all lunch period for from Deidre.

"So, Clara. Why were you and Eli late to Menendez this morning? You both came in way after the bell rang."

I felt Tate tense beside me. Deidre was jealous. She apparently had a crush on Tate forever and decided to tell me this after I'd already been going out with him for weeks. Then she expected me to dump him because of it, just like that. I explained to her she should have said something before. She was still pissed, hence the foul behavior from her. She was pretty - really pretty. She tanned every week and had a bright glow to her that matched her more strawberry than blonde hair perfectly. But it didn't match her demeanor.

"We were late because Eli saved me," I told everyone.

"What?" she sneered in unbelief.

"What?" Tate bellowed, his jealously gone. "Saved you from what?"

"Some big freshman guy slapped me on the behind in the hall when I accidentally bumped him," I explained. "Eli put him in his place."

"*Behind*? What are you? Two?" Deidre sneered but everyone ignored her.

"What? Who?" Tate said louder.

"I don't know, but Eli handled it."

Tate looked at Eli and nodded to him.

"Thanks, man. I owe ya."

"No worries. I was glad to help."

Tate nodded again and then turned to me once everyone started talking about their own 'brushes with death'.

"I should have walked you to Menendez, I forgot about the delinquent hall."

Our in-school suspension was on that hall and it was always full.

"It's ok. You would have never made it to Shop if you had."

I heard Dee making gagging noises.

"Well, I'll walk you tomorrow. I'll explain to Bishop. He'll understand or I'll just be late everyday."

"I can walk her if you want. We have the same class," Eli offered easily and yawned into his fist like he was bored.

"Uh..." I knew Tate was absolutely not thrilled with that. "Well, tomorrow, sure. Then I should be able to do it after that."

"Guys," Dee groaned. "You act like she's a precious little movie star or something whose adoring fans are getting rough. She's fine. So one guy grabbed her butt, big deal. I think she's blowing all this a little out of proportion anyway."

"Shut up, Dee," Tate said.

"No, she's right," I said and looked right at her then back to Tate. "It's ok. I'll be fine."

"I want someone to walk you, Clara," he insisted.

"Who's gonna walk me?" Dee asked snidely. "I have that same class."

"Yeah, but you come up to it from your locker on the East wing, Clara's locker is on the South. You don't even touch delinquent hall and it'd take too long for her to walk around it."

She pouted and looked hurt. I knew better. Witch.

"Are you ok?" Tate asked quietly. "Did he hurt you?"

"No. I'm fine."

"You're sure? I'm sure I can find out who this guy is. I'll make sure he understands not to-"

"I'm fine. Really," I soothed and put my hand on his leg. "So, what time is your match?"

"Uh....five. You're coming right?"

"Yep. I love to see you hug sweaty men. It really does it for me," I said sarcastically but with a sweet smile plastered on.

"Aww," he crooned and pinched my cheek. "What a thoughtful girlfriend."

I laughed and leaned in to kiss him quickly but he pulled me back to him, keeping me there and once again, kissing me in front of the whole school, which he never did. I had a feeling this had a lot to do with Eli but I would never accuse of him of such.

With his hand on my cheek I let him kiss me. When I heard our friends start to comment and joke, I pulled back and licked my lips before looking up, straight to Eli.

He was looking between ecstasy and pain. It was strange how he got that look but this time he didn't seem to be enjoying it, whatever it was; like it was something he had to do but didn't like it.

When he saw me looking he quickly schooled his features into neutral and began studying his food, but I was intrigued now to say the least. I looked back up to Tate to see smug satisfaction as he threw his arm over my shoulder. He was content for the moment and that was good enough for me.

"So, babe. Wanna do something after the match? We can go to Snitzy's."

"Yes!" Deidre chimed loudly like her say was final. "Let's all go to Snitzy's after the match."

"I meant me and you," he muttered softly to me, but we both knew better than to mess with Deidre.

"Bell's about to ring," Mike said.

"Crap," Tate said sitting up. "I gotta go all the way to the back lot so I'm gonna take off." He looked at me. "See you in the stands?"

"I'll be there."

He kissed me quickly and shot up from his seat, striding across the lunchroom with a smile. Our group quickly dispersed from there. I asked Eli about the rest of his schedule. We had every class together after lunch.

Great.

So, we walked together. I told him about the wrestling match tonight and asked if he wanted to come. My friends had been friendly enough to him. Sarah still giggled at him and made flirty jokes about his accent. He said he would like to go and I told him where and when.

We were assigned alphabetically in the next class, Math, so we didn't get to sit beside each other; which was probably for the best anyway. It went by quickly as we were given our books and an outline of our curriculum for the year. Then our next and last class of the day was Art. We walked together again.

I told myself it was to show him where it was but I could foresee us walking together everyday. Why not?

Art was a laid back - sit wherever - do whatever - kinda thing. I moseyed nonchalantly to the back and took a corner work desk. It was a two seater, kind of like a lab desk. Eli came to stand beside me and I couldn't tell if I was happy or not about the fact that he was going to ask to sit down.

"Do you think I could sit here, or would Tate not be happy about that?"

"Um..." I stalled.

"Alright. Just thought I'd ask even though I already knew the answer," he said and turned to go.

I bit my lip. This was ridiculous. Tate couldn't tell me who to be friends with.

"Wait," I called. "It's fine."

"Don't feel sorry for me. I can sit somewhere else, it's fine. I just figured it'd be more fun to sit with you."

"I don't feel sorry for you. I *want* you to sit. I never get to pair off with anyone I know for these things."

"You're sure? I don't want to get you in trouble."

I bristled at his implication but knew it wasn't really him I was upset about. If Tate hadn't showed his butt last night, Eli would have no reason to think that.

"No, I promise. It's fine."

He sat down, taking off his bag and throwing it over the edge of the chair. I didn't want things to be weird so I started talking right away.

"So. Where did you go to school before? Did you go to where your parents taught?"

"Yep. Over there kids of all ages sit in the same classroom. It was weird I guess. It was kind of like being homeschooled. It was very laid back and they tried to make it fun."

"That's sounds cool. So why did you move to the states?"

"Back to the states, actually," he clarified. "We lived in Seattle until I was twelve. Then moved to Zimbabwe until now. Now I'm eighteen, graduating and they'll be leaving for some other place soon and I'll have to figure out what I want to do."

"I hear you there. I'm so lost on what to do with the rest of my life."

"What do your parents do?" he asked, putting his head on his elbow to look at me.

"They died a few months ago," I answered smoothly and tried to keep the sting out of my voice.

That response always elicited mixed responses from people and I tried to not make it uncomfortable for them by tearing up.

"Ah, man, I'm sorry."

I shrugged. It wasn't like I could say 'it's ok' because it wasn't, but I could at least try to keep it together.

The teacher came in and started to explain our goals for the year. To create a piece for submission to any art school of our choice, whether we wanted to go to Art school or not, was our final grade.

"And today, we'll be learning about shading. No piddling in my class. We'll be starting right out of the gate with a graded project due by the end of class."

The collective groan of the class was lost on me. I was excited. Art was exciting and fun and with Eli as my table partner, I had a feeling it would be interesting this year.

"I'm sorry I brought up your parents," he said and looked up at me a moment before looking back to his paper.

"It's ok that you did. You couldn't have known," I said and felt my heart break a little at having to say that. "I want to remember them. It's nice to talk about them sometimes. Everyone else avoids it because they think it'll make me sad."

Having to tell someone they were allowed to bring my parents up... It was just wrong. I looked at Eli and saw that same expression on his face as before. Ecstasy wrapped in pain and discomfort.

"Are you ok?" I asked.

"Yes," he answered, his voice strained. "I'm fine, just uh..." He looked at me and I felt bad. I had made him uncomfortable with all that dead parent talk and now he was embarrassed or something. I felt even worse. And then his face twisted even more. "I've got to go," he said suddenly and huskily.

"What? Class just started?" I protested, completely baffled.

"I'll see you tonight, ok? At the match," he called as he grabbed his stuff and made a swift getaway out the classroom door.

I was so very confused, but what could I do? I didn't have his number to check on him. He'd been acting kind of weird all day. I would ask him tonight.

Maybe he was going through something or having a problem about moving again.

Class ended uneventfully and I turned my shade in of a Dogwood tree along the river bank to which the teacher smiled at me me in appreciation. I made my way across the street quickly and prepared for the barrage of screams and squeals.

"Clara! Clara's home!" Josiah announced loudly, as he did everyday.

"Clawa!" Hannah yelled happily and wrapped herself around my leg. "I had fishies today."

"You did," I crooned and picked her up, slating her to my hip. "Oh, man. I could really chow down on some gold fishies right now."

"There's more! In there!" she pointed towards the kitchen and I followed her instruction. "Mommy, mommy! Clawa wants fishies too!"

"Oh does she now?" Ruth said and smiled at me. "Hi, Clara. How was school today?"

"Great. I can handle my new classes pretty well. And there was a new guy today. Eli, from Zimbabwe."

"Really? That's interesting. What was he doing there?"

"He said his parents were some kind of teaching missionaries or something."

"That's awesome. God Bless them. Now, honey, would you mind taking this stack of letters to the post office on your way to the match tonight? I didn't make it today and it's the get well cards for the church members."

"Sure. No problem."

"You're such a sweet girl. You know we love having you around, don't you?"

"Yes, ma'am, I do, and I like being here too."

"Good. Have fun tonight and you know Pastor's rules."

"No after midnight and don't do anything I wouldn't do if he was watching me."

"That's our girl. Everybody say, have fun Clara."

A sweet shrill untamed chorus of 'have fun Clara' rang out as I smiled and ran to my room in the back of the hall. The parish was a small but pretty green cottage type house right next to the church. It was one story but I got lucky, my room was all the way on the other side of the house so I never heard babies crying at night.

I took a quick shower and went to put on some clothes. I had to be at the games and matches half an hour early to sell hats and buttons and ribbons and such.

I picked out a red long sleeve shirt and jeans with my black boots, to match our school colors for The Red Devils.

It was getting chilly out at night now but I figured long sleeves were good enough. I fixed my hair in the mirror on my dresser. My room, my temporary room, was cute. It had been Mrs. Ruth's sewing room but when I moved in, she let me have it because there was no where else to go. The walls were a pastel purple and the trim and carpet was a lime green. She'd asked me several times if I wanted to paint or change anything, but I figured I wouldn't be here that long and I wanted to make it as easy on them as possible when I left to get things back to normal.

Once I was ready, I headed downstairs and said my goodbyes before walking down to the post office and then hurrying across the street to the school and around back to the gym. Sarah already had our table set up and was putting out all our merchandise. She was the only one of my friends who participated in the sprit squad, or anything really. The boys were into their sports but Dee and Meagan refused anything extracurricular for school.

"Hey! Ready to sell the mess outta some t-shirts? Mrs. Collins said if we don't sell the t-shirts tonight, she won't order anymore. I say we kiss whoever buys one. They'll sell like hotcakes."

"You go right ahead," I told her laughing. "I'll stick to the buttons and mugs."

Sarah was the quirky friend. She wore these outrageous outfits and her crazy curly red hair was always bunched into some kinda wild bun or pigtails. She was so very pretty and guys liked her because she was fun and outgoing, and her skirts were usually shorter than they should be.

Within no time, the people started pouring in and I saw Eli. He looked casual and did a subtle double take when he saw me. He smiled and made his way over to me, but Sarah intercepted him. I couldn't hear them because her back was to me, but I saw her put her hand on his arm and I felt a flare of something strange go through me. Jealousy? Me? No...

I looked back up to see Eli watching me with a slightly shocked expression. He seemed almost pleased about something and it irked me even more, though he was looking at me not Sarah. But I had no right or claim to him. I had a boyfriend and felt bad enough as it was. I wiped those thoughts away and concentrated on the people flowing by.

"So, anyway," she was saying as she walked towards me with her arm in his. "I sit in the middle behind the home team. I'll find you when I'm done, ok?"

"Alright," he said smoothly and detangled himself from her. "Clara, hey."

Sarah bristled and a frown appeared as she heard his tone. She huffed silently and turned to take care of a customer.

"Hey, you made it."

"I told you I would."

"Listen. Are you ok? You seem to be acting a little...strange, and you ran out of class today. I've never been the new kid before, but I'm sure it sucks."

"It's not that. I'm just going through something, I guess." He stuck his hands in his pockets. "I'm sorry if I was rude."

"No. No, I was just worried about you," I assured and turned the ring on my finger to keep from looking at him.

"You were worried about me," he repeated and smiled crookedly at me.

"Yeah...ok. Well, we'll be done here in a few minutes. We'll join you, if you want to sit with us," I said, giving him an out if he wanted it.

"Yeah," he said softly and flicked his eyes to the table. "And I'll take a...hmm. What's a big selling item?"

"Mugs and buttons are our biggest."

"What's your lamest?"

"T-shirts."

"Well them I'll take a t-shirt."

I laughed and picked through them to find his size and took his ten dollars. "You want the lamest item? Why? Trying to go against the flow?" I joked.

"Nope, just don't want the t-shirt to feel left out," he said and winked before walking away.

"OMG. He was so flirting with you," Sarah said loudly and I shh'ed her.

"No, he's not. You're just like Tate. Just because a guy talks to me doesn't mean he wants to date me, ok?"

"Yeah, but I want to date him and he wants to date you. I can tell these things."

"Well then get your radar checked," I yelled playfully. "Everyone needs to get over it. I'm dating Tate, end of story."

"Well it better be. You already got a hunk!" she chimed. "Well, let me sit next to him when we go out there, ok? I need a little help. Maybe I came on too strong earlier," she mused and bit her thumb nail.

"You? Never," I said, my sarcasm dripping.

We laughed as we put up our wares and made our way to the packed bleachers. It seemed the whole town came out for these things. I let Sarah sit next to Eli and other than a quick look from him, I received no reaction. Once we sat down I remembered that I hadn't had any supper and was going to get a hotdog. I turned to Sarah to say as much, but Eli stood and waved me off.

"I'll get it. I was going anyway."

"Ok, great, thanks."

"You want anything, Sarah?" he asked politely.

"Diet Coke, no ice, please."

"Sure thing."

As soon as he was gone she leaned over and put her head on my shoulder dreamily.

"His eyes. Oh my gosh, those eyes! Have you seen them? The most gorgeous purple eyes ever."

Yes, I wanted to say. Yes, I'd seen his gorgeous eyes. In fact, I saw them first. But I held my tongue and looked out to see Tate about to take the mat. As Sarah droned on in my ear about Eli's accent, Tate looked for me and when he found me he smiled. He made kiss lips at me, too, making Sarah produce gagging noises beside me. I punched her arm playfully and she laughed before starting a chant for our team. Eli came back a couple minutes later with our food and drinks and passed them out before taking a seat...next to me.

I heard Sarah huff beside me and I tried not to giggle. I glanced at Eli and he was smiling like he knew a secret.

We watched the match and I finished my hotdog in record time. Sarah was going on and on about the opposing team. About how hot Tate's wrestling opponent was and how she was going to get his number after the match. Eli was forgotten, just like that.

The match didn't last long. We won, of course, and Mike and Deidre finally made their way over to us.

"Hey, guys. Snitzy's right? Let's go get a burger," Mike reminded.

"We just ate," Sarah groaned, but then changed her expression to a smile. "But I'd love to go and hang out. Eli, you in?"

"Are you in?" he asked me and I saw Deidre put a hand on her hip in my peripheral.

"Yeah. It's still early. My curfew's midnight."

"Then I'm in," he answered and smiled slightly at me.

Deidre pushed Mike aside, squeezed herself towards us and then plopped herself on Eli's lap. Eli remained still and expressionless as he watched me. When she wound her arms around his neck, I closed my eyes and shook my head as I looked away.

"So," Dee started, "Clara, why don't you go get your boyfriend?"

"I'm sure he's coming."

"Well then let's go. I'm riding with Eli."

Being able to tolerate Dee was getting harder by the minute. So I got up without a word and walked to the locker room. Tate was all showered and changed, checking his phone when I came up. I apparently startled him because he looked shocked at seeing me. He put his phone away quickly, like he'd been waiting for a call or text maybe.

"What's up? Are you ok?" I asked.

"Yeah. I was about to text you, but here you are." He kissed my cheek and threw an arm around my shoulder. "What's up with you? You never come to the locker rooms after matches."

"Everybody wants to go eat, remember? You still wanna come with us?"

"Everybody who?"

"Mike, Dee, Eli-"

"Ok. Cool."

We all piled into Tate's truck and Mike's car and made our way across town. Dee and Eli rode in the back seat of the truck with us and I heard Dee trying to coax him into taking her out this weekend. He didn't say much, but once when I glanced back, she had her lips on his chin, nipping playfully and then kissing it. Eli and my eyes locked for a second before I looked away.

Tate pulled me from the seat out his door once we arrived. He seemed anxious or riled up. Maybe it was from the match. He held my hand a little too tightly. I looked at him funny and he smirked and kissed my fingers as we waited for everyone else to order. Tate ordered me an iced coffee and himself a big burger with the works. We sat scattered around two pushed together tables and listened to the country playing on the radio above us screaming some Taylor Swift song.

For some reason my eyes kept drifting to Dee and Eli. He seemed so disinterested, so why did he let her touch him and carry on like that? Every time I looked his way, he was already looking at me. You'd think I'd be creeped out or feel weird about it but, it felt almost welcome to me. It was strange why I was so ok with it, but I knew I had to let this go...whatever this little attraction to Eli was. So when Tate started touching me, I completely opened myself up to it and tried to feel every sensation it gave me. I wanted to be full of Tate, my boyfriend.

I ran my hand up his thigh after he did the same to me. I played with his fingers as his thumb caressed my wrist. When he leaned over to peck the side of my neck, as he did often, I leaned back to him and kissed his jaw, my hand gripping his arm. He looked at me with a pleased, but surprised face. He pulled me to sit in his lap.

"What's gotten into you?" he whispered amusedly in my ear.

"What? You don't want me to?"

"Oh, I want you to. You're just usually not like this."

"Well, I want to play tonight," I said and bit my lip. "Is that wrong?"

He grinned and pulled my face to his, his lips were greedy and I tasted alcohol. Someone had brought a flask with them and the guys had spiked their drinks. Great. I didn't stop though, there was no point. I ran my hands through his hair and let him kiss me. I stopped him once his hand tried to slide too far up my thigh.

"Clara," he growled quietly in my ear. "You are such a tease." I looked at him, but he was smiling a little. "One of these days..."

He seemed a little more frustrated with the brakes than usual. I wondered about it, but let it go.

When the girl brought our food, I cringed, knowing exactly what was coming.

"Hey, Molly. Nice costume. You know it's not Halloween yet, but you get points for showing up early," Dee sneered and the expected heckling and laughing followed.

Molly was one our school Goths. She worked at this burger joint that we loved to come to and Dee and the rest of them always gave her crap every time we came.

"Bite me, Deidre. You couldn't pull off black anyway."

"Oh, you're right about that. I'm not dead."

"Yet," Molly said and smiled brightly before bouncing off.

Dee fumed and huffed. "Eli, did you hear what she said to me?"

"Yep," he answered easily.

"Well?" she replied indignantly.

"Well?" he said and drug it out to be sarcastic.

"You're not going to do anything about it? She practically threatened me!" she yelled and put a hand on her chest to barter some sympathy.

"That sounds like a job for a boyfriend to me."

She scoffed as Mike and Tom laughed. I saw her turn red, but then she switched and smiled, albeit fake.

"Ah, is that your way of asking me to go out with you? So sweet," she said and kissed his cheek from behind, wrapping her arms around his neck.

He didn't comment and didn't look at her, only me. I started to wonder why no one noticed that he'd pretty much stared at me all night.

Before Molly returned, Dee orchestrated revenge, as always. She poured her water glass on the floor next to her chair. When Molly came, Dee specifically complained about her burger and asked her to come view the hair in plain sight. When she did, she slipped and fell on her butt, right there in front of everyone, including other customers.

"Oopsy! That's a Workman's Comp. claim right there," Dee said seriously then burst out laughing and the minions followed suit.

"Yeah, Molls," Mike yelled. "I'd watch it. You're gonna flatten out that back side even more. We'll have to change your name to no-butt."

I stayed quiet as I always did as they cackled like hyenas around me, and so did Eli. Molly got up, red faced and embarrassed and stalked behind the counter. When she came to give us our ticket, Mike asked her how her fall had been. It must have hurt, he said, because she had no padding to break it and then he tried to grab her butt…again. Molly just slammed the ticket on the table and left. They didn't leave a tip, they never did.

I threw a couple dollars down as I walked out, but it wasn't nearly enough for a group our size.

Tate dropped me off at home and Eli got out as well, saying he could walk, it wasn't far. Tate kissed me and then saluted Eli.

"Go straight in the house, Clara. It's late, ok?" Tate ordered.

"Sure."

"Alright. I'm gonna run Dee home. See you tomorrow, babe."

"Bye."

Dee climbed over the seat to sit in the front with Tate as he drove off and I turned to Eli.

"They're fun, huh?" I said sarcastically, knowing he didn't really have fun.

"Yeah, a blast," he said wryly.

"Ok, well-"

"So do you guys always hang out like that? Just sitting around different venues...making fun of people?" he said and I thought I heard a bit of an accusation in there.

"Pretty much. That's all they ever do. I hate it. I wish I'd never went with them at all once I'm there."

"Then why go?"

"Something to do? Routine? Bored? That's all I got. Take your pick."

"Hmm."

"So you and Dee?" I asked cautiously.

"Nope."

I was confused.

"But you let her hang all over you? She kissed you," I said and groaned inside at sounding jealous even to my ears.

"I was testing...someone. To see if they'd react to another girl showing interest in me."

That sounded cryptic and loony, but it almost made sense.

"Well? What did you find out?"

"Oh, she reacts," he said wryly, pushing his fingers through his hair.

"Is it how you wanted her to?"

"Not quite. She's made a habit of making out with her boyfriend more often to ward off the attraction. It's kind of backfiring actually," he said with a little smile and crossed his arms over his chest.

My mouth opened, but no words came. He was talking about me. How had I not seen that one coming? Oh, I know. Because he was ruggedly handsome and exotic and different and he knew I had a boyfriend.

I just smiled shyly and turned to go. "Bye, Eli. See you tomorrow."

"Bye, Clara," he floated my name on his breath. "Sweet…dreams."

And sweet dreams was what I had. Even though I wasn't asleep, when I closed my eyes it was like another world was waiting behind my eyelids. Tonight, the dark boy and I met in the school cafeteria. I should have been scared. The last time we'd met I got a feeling of being terrified, but had no reason to be and didn't understand it. I wasn't scared now.

I found myself just walking around the dark dreary room, completely pitch black except wide streams of moon and streetlight beaming in. It was funny how our perception of everything changed by just the time of day changing. At night everything seemed so much more mysterious. I was in my sleep clothes this time; a pair of sleep shorts with little penguins on them and a black off the shoulder t-shirt.

I didn't see him anywhere yet, but I had a feeling he would be here, so I just walked around, thinking about all the times I'd eaten there and all the stupid things my 'friends' had done.

"What are you thinking about?" I heard him say behind me. "You're concentrating pretty hard."

I turned to see him sitting on the tabletop, half in the shadows a few tables away.

"I'm just wondering who you are, and why I feel strange around you."

"Strange how?"

"Strange like...I don't know. Like I should be afraid, but I'm not. I trust you but I don't even know you."

"What if you did know me? Would that help things?"

"Would you still come to me when I closed my eyes?"

"Yes."

"Then I don't know. I guess I'd feel like I was cheating on my boyfriend. I shouldn't be thinking about other guys."

"But it's not real, right?" he said and his tone indicated he didn't believe it.

"Why does it feel so real?"

He ignored my question and asked me one.

"Why are you so sad?"

"What?"

"The sorrow...it's pouring off you."

I sat down on the table top like him, but I was still a table away. "My parents died not too long ago. I'm not over it."

"I'm sorry. That must be tough."

"It is. Or it was. It's not so bad now I just miss them. I live with a really great family."

He seemed to absorb that answer. Then he spoke again and leaned back even further in the shadows.

"I wish I could take it all from you; your sadness, your sorrow. I'd want you to never feel pain again if I had the say in it."

"Thanks, but everyone has to feel those things at some point. It's what makes us who we are...makes us human."

"You are a remarkable person. I can't wait to get to know you. I want to know everything about you."

"Everything?" I laughed. "There's not much to know. So, are you.... are you going to scare me again, like last night?" I asked and felt bold and blunt. I wanted to go to him, but knew there was some unspoken boundary there.

"No. No more scaring. That was a mistake, one I regret and apologize for. Had I known then what I know now, things would have gone differently."

"What do you know now?"

"That I am completely and utterly taken by you. I can't function without you invading my mind, day and night."

"I have a boyfriend," I said though I knew he knew.

"Yes, I know. But can he invade your subconscious?" he said and I heard the smile in his voice.

"No," I whispered. "Can I see your face?"

"Does it matter what I look like to you?"

"No, but I want to know the face to look at in my mind when I remember this later."

He chuckled. "One day," he promised. "There are a few things I have to take care of first."

"What's that?"

I didn't hear or see him move, but I felt his breath on my neck and his voice in my ear saying, "All in good time, Clara."

~ ~ ~

The next day was a repeat of the first, minus bullies on the way to Menendez. Tate let Eli walk me to class and it was all fine. He talked to Bishop about it and he said it wasn't his problem. So, begrudged, Tate asked Eli to walk me to class everyday if he didn't mind.

We all met at the school that night for another match. Dee, Megan, Sarah, Eli, Mike and I sat in the bleachers and watched as the guys warmed up and sparred in preparation.

Dee worked overtime to get Eli's attention as he and Mike talked about our football team and how Eli should sign up. Eli avoided her a lot more and once, he leaned forward to put his elbows on his knees while he watched the first match start and she rubbed his back. He shrugged her hand off and turned to look at me. It was like he was telling me he was done pretending with her. His case was made and he was waiting on me.

But all was forgotten soon when Tate started acting funny. Even if you didn't know him you could see something was wrong. He was shaking his head from side to side furiously when he took his stance and his face was as red and twisted as I ever seen it.

I heard Eli take a deep startled breath beside me and the look was back. This time there was no painful look involved. Eli was just soaking in whatever it was he was doing. Pure ecstasy and goodness was all over his face as he watched the boys face off. It made me stiffen with concern and curiosity, but Tate was taking my focus right then.

Then Tate did the thing that matched the face he was wearing. He threw the boy on the mat and with a cry of battle rage began to smash the guys face with his fists, over and over. It seemed he'd hit him at least ten times before someone reached them to stop him. Tate was straining and yelling for them to let him go; he was bloodthirsty. The crowd all stood in silent shock. The boy was bleeding from many places and groaning as he rolled on the mat in obvious pain.

Without thought, I stepped down the bleachers and went to Tate as he struggled with coach. I touched his arm and started to say his name, hoping to calm him.

"Ta-" I said, but he reached and punched me hard in the chest with a fist that got free.

I fell back forcefully to the mat on my back and heard a big gasp from the onlookers. I rubbed the spot he'd hit and felt the sting of it. I looked around shocked and realized what had just happened. Tate had just pushed me down in front of the entire school and half the town.

Three

I was stunned as I looked up to him and saw him finally register it, too. His whole face changed and he looked so incredibly guilty.

The other coach, Mr. Mackey, came to help me up. He kept his arm around me, for support or courage to pass Tate, I wasn't sure which, but as we passed him Tate spoke to me in a gut wrenchingly heartbreaking voice.

"Clara, I didn't mean to. I didn't know it was you. Please, babe, I'd never hurt you. You know that."

I didn't say anything, just walked. I didn't know what to say.

"I'll call your parents," coach Mackey said and then blanched. "I mean, the Pastor."

"No, It's ok. I just live across the street. I can make it."

"I'll make sure she gets home safely," I heard behind me and saw Eli there, a grim and unhappy look on his face.

"Alright, Mr. Thames. Good of you. Go on then. We'll take care of Tate, you just get on home."

"Yes, sir," I answered and let Eli lead me away, a thousand eyes on me, with his hand on my lower back. Once we reached the parking lot I finally felt the weight of the situation. "Oh my- what just happened?" I whispered hoarsely, my hands on my cheeks.

"What happened was your junkie boyfriend hit you," he said angrily. "Are you ok?"

I rubbed the spot on my chest and winced as the sting.

"Yeah, I'm ok. Wait- junkie? What do you mean?" I asked hotly and stood with him by the gate to the school entrance.

"I mean he's using steroids. He's got classic hot head syndrome."

"Steroids," I whispered and shook my head back and forth furiously. "No. No, he wouldn't."

"So he'd just hit you for no reason?" When I didn't answer he leaned over me, placing his hands on the bars above me, towering over me. "Has he done this before, Clara?"

"No, never. He's always been gentle with me."

"Has he ever beat a guy like that before?"

"No."

"I'm sorry, Clara, but I think he's got a problem. State is coming up isn't it? Wrestling is a really big deal in this town," he said with inflection.

I stayed silent as I looked out at nothing in the dark. I mentally waded through his behavior lately. He'd been very snappy, even with me, and his dad, the mayor, was on him more than anyone about making his town proud. Oh no, it was true.

"I want you to be wrong," I confessed softly.

"I want to be, too, but I don't think I am," he said just as softly.

The moon was shining streaks of white through his dark hair and his brow ring caught the light, twinkling. I reached up and touched it before I even realized what I was doing. He shivered and I finally looked into his eyes that were already watching me. His eyes were so violet, even in the night, and they captured me. I could literally have stood there all night and just locked gazes with him and smelled him. This close, he smelled like soap and something else, something delicious.

His face took on that familiar twist of enjoyment, but he seemed to keep in reigned in for the most part.

His hand came down to smooth my cheek. "Are you ok? You seem very...torn," he said finally.

I could think of nothing with his hand on me. Absolutely no words came to mind as I just stood there and let him touch me and held his gaze. And then he leaned in slightly, carefully, testing me. More, more. Then when he was so close I felt his breath on my lips, I put a hand on his chest to stop him.

"I'm sorry," I whispered. "I can't."

"Because of Tate?" he asked and I heard the edge there.

"Yes."

"He hit you, Clara," he growled. "He hurt you. How can you even think about him right now?"

"I know what Tate just did was horrible, but I have to talk to him. I can't kiss you when I'm still dating someone else, even if it is on the rocks. I'm not like that."

He nodded and seemed to calm down.

"All right. You're right. I respect that." He leaned back and took a deep breath. "Come on. I'll get you home."

~ ~ ~

Pastor was waiting on the porch for me. "Coach called. You ok?" he said and came to pull me into a hug.

"I'm fine. Pastor, this is Eli Thames. He's new."

"Thank you, son, for walking her home," Pastor said and shook his hand.

"No problem, sir. I'm glad to help."

"Well, you need a ride home?"

"I just live a little bit that way," he pointed and started making his way. "See you tomorrow, Clara."

"Bye. And thank you," I called.

He nodded and lifted a hand in acknowledgement as he walked away.

Pastor took me inside and passed me to Mrs. Ruth, who took me straight down the hall for an inspection. She removed my shirt and even through my bra I could see a faint spot showing right between my breasts.

"Clara...I can't believe Tate did this to you. I think it's needless to say you can't see him anymore and we need to file a police report."

"No! Wait... He didn't know it was me, I came up behind him. I need to talk to him first, to understand what happened."

"Clara...I don't think it's a good idea, but...I'll talk to Pastor about it." She ran her hand down the back of my hair. "You want to stay home from school tomorrow? I'm sure that would be quite all right."

"It's ok. People will just talk even worse if I'm not there. They'll say Tate killed me or something," I joked and tried to make light of it. "I'll go, I'm fine."

"If you're sure. I'll make you pancakes in the morning, ok?"

"Mrs. Ruth, it's ok. I know the twins keep you up at night. Really, I'm fine. You guys are doing just fine at taking care of me. You don't have to try so hard," I said with a smile.

"Oh, honey. It's been a pleasure having you stay with us. Your parents are so proud of you. I guarantee it."

"Thanks."

"Night. Let me know if you need anything. You know I'll be up," she said wryly making me laugh.

"Ok, thank you."

She closed the door and left. I collapsed on my bed, wondering how the day had ended like it had. Pulling my knees up I felt the sting in my chest and buried my head under my pillow. He hadn't known it was me coming up behind him...but still. Why would he punch someone he when he didn't even know who it was? Just because it was me still didn't make it ok for it to be someone else.

I lay down just like that, my bra on and jeans, face under my silk pillow case and feet hanging off the side of the bed. I closed my eyes and realized my subconscious had been invaded when I was standing back at the school gate. I was leaning my back against it and there was a presence over me. It wasn't ominous, though I felt if it had been seen by someone else they would have thought so. He leaned in, his face shaded and dark like before, his breath overly warm and powerful before my lips. He spoke.

"I've waited a very long time for you. Please don't hate me."

"Why would I hate you?" I whispered, fearing my voice would no longer work.

"I'm not a good person. I'm an evil thing that has fallen under your spell," he muttered and ran the back of his hand down my cheek and neck.

"Eli?" I asked, testing my theory.

"Is that who you want it to be?"

"I want you to be who you are."

He hesitated, then the shadow lifted from his face as he inched closer and I was struck by his face. He was unlike anything I'd ever seen. He looked like him, but not. He was so completely breathtaking with his gorgeous ruggedness and imperfections and he was looking at me like I was the only thing he wanted in this whole world.

"What did you mean you're an evil thing, Eli?" I asked.

"I am...something I can't describe. I'm not worthy of you in any sense of the word, but I must have you. Do you understand? You have ensnared me, bewitched me, and I can no longer exist without you with me."

"I barely know you," I whispered.

"But I know you," he said cryptically against my cheek, kissing my scorching flesh. "Open your eyes, sleeping beauty."

I gasped aware on my bed and felt my cheek where he had laid his soft lips. It was still too warm to be normal. I sat up and looked around. Oh, man. My imagination was working overtime. Was I becoming one of those pathetic girls who couldn't get a boy off her mind to the point of obsession, usually ending in restraining orders and timed served at a mental health facility?

When I lay back down and closed my eyes, I was alone.

The next morning I woke with a start. A quick glance at the clock showed I was borderline running late so I hurried to jump in the shower. The bruise was a little more angry today, but still not horrible. I put my hair up in a ponytail and worried over my wardrobe. I'd have to pick something to hide the bruise. I put on my black turtleneck under my school vest and earrings with a necklace so I didn't look like I was trying to cover anything up.

I was just normal me. The mirror said as much and I grabbed my bag swiftly from the chair and raced downstairs. I kissed all the babies and grabbed an apple as I shoved my way out the door, trailing loud goodbyes in my wake.

Once I reached the street though, I was suddenly overcome with a sense of embarrassment and shame. What had happened last night would no doubt be the talk of the school today. My steps faltered and I looked around at all the faces. There seemed to be a lot of eyes trained on me but then looking away quickly. I straightened my back and slung my bag further up my shoulder.

I was not going to cower for something I didn't even do.

I walked all the way across the street and saw a few people who normally didn't talk to me wave at me and smile. I returned it and looked for my friends. I saw Megan and Deidre...with Eli. Deidre had her tacky fake nails on his arm and was pushing her chest against him as she laughed at whatever he was saying.

And just like he could sense me, Eli looked up and directly at me. He watched me watch him and then he craned his neck, his expression changing, and began to come forward but Dee grabbed his arm to stop him. I wondered what was wrong but then I felt it. The warm, gentle hand on my wrist and the eerie quiet of the courtyard as everyone watched.

Tate.

"Hey. I'm glad you came today. I was so worried about you last night but you're phone was dead and the Pastor wouldn't get you for the house phone."

"I'm surprised you came," I said softly.

"Why? I had to see you," he said and came closer, his hand drifting down to rest in mine.

I heard a bunch of murmurs and gasps and looked around to see everyone's eyes still glued to us. I pulled him by his arm, feeling Eli's eyes on me, and took a swift glance to confirm that. He looked like he wanted to follow, but I towed Tate all the way through the school to the girls bathroom. I shut the door and turned against it for support as I faced him.

"What's wrong, Tate?

"Nothing," he said and looked at the floor. "I'm fine. I just got really mad. That guy was cheating."

"Don't lie to me. Not to me." He took a deep breath before letting his book bag fall to the floor and shoving his hands in his pockets. "Steroids, Tate? Really?"

"You don't know what it's like!" he yelled and I flinched.

He saw and came until he was flush with my toes. He touched my cheek. "You can't think I'd ever hurt you. I'd never, ever, hurt you, Clara. I love you."

He finally said it. After he hit me and humiliated me in front of the whole school, he says it.

"Tate, I can't do this. You can't just say, 'yes I'm taking steroids' and expect everything to just go back to normal. Stop taking them!" I yelled and he seemed surprise by it. "Get your crap back together! You could have killed that guy! Do you even understand that?"

"I know, ok!" he yelled back. "I know, but what can I do about it now? I already got a court date for it. Friday I have to see a judge and them tell me what they're gonna do to me. That guy pressed charges so..."

"As he should have, Tate. You really hurt him."

"My mom was worried you were going to press charges, too," he muttered and looked at me from under his lashes. I noticed his parents weren't worried about me, just Tate's reputation.

"Pastor wants me to, but I told them I had to talk to you first."

"That's my girl," he crooned, cracking a smile and pulling me to him. "I knew you'd know I never meant to hurt you. It was an accident."

I pushed him back a little. "This isn't over, just like that. You hurt me, Tate, and scared me. Watching you hit that guy over and over...I never want to see that again. That's not who you are."

"I know it's not. I'm sorry. Babe, I'm so sorry. I love you, please, please, forgive me," he begged into my neck.

"I'm working on it," I told him. "But you have to stop taking them."

"Already did. I flushed it all last night when I got home. I'm done, babe. Promise."

"Good."

I let him kiss me, though I wasn't into it, he didn't seem to notice. I noticed he never asked to see my bruise or if there even was one. And after a few minutes we made our way, well passed the bell, into the empty hall and he walked me to my first period class. He opened the door for me and kissed me right in front of everyone as they all looked to see who was coming in late. My cheeks flashed scarlet and I wanted to ask Tate why he had done that. It was like he was telling everyone 'See, she forgave me, ha!'

The rest of the week went just like that. Tate was extra attentive, especially in the halls where everyone could see. Our group of friends pretended that nothing had happened at all and everything was fine. And Eli.

When I lay down at night and closed my eyes, Eli was right there, every night. The first night he pulled the collar of my shirt down with his finger to see my bruise and winced. He said he'd kill him if I'd let him. We almost kissed every time and he always told me he needed me and wanted me more than anyone else. In real life, he was different.

He watched me, always watching, and Deidre seemed to cling to him whether he wanted her to or not and he let her, but everyone could tell he was just humoring her. I heard her say he was taking her out on Saturday, but who knew if that was true, knowing Dee. He never spoke to me unless it was about school stuff as he walked with me to classes and in Art. Things were strange, awkward in an oddly comfortable way. It seemed that Eli was just waiting for me. And I was curious about the dream-like visits and how I felt so strange around him.

And Tate. He had spent every night at my house. Despite Pastors' advice, I let him come over and told them everything was fine. It was all just a big misunderstanding. They didn't seem convinced, but let me have it anyway. Tate tried to seduce me in his truck before we went in every night. I told him he didn't have to try to make up for anything anymore. He said he wasn't, he just wanted me so badly. I had to physically push him to stop him twice, which I'd never had to do before.

He said he wanted to come walk me to school the next day so I let him. He pulled up in his truck but instead of walking he lifted me onto the seat and climbed in beside me. He drove into the parking lot of the school and parked. Then he pulled me onto his lap immediately and began frantically kissing me. He kissed my neck and tugged my hair to pull my head back to give him more access to my throat. He moaned and groaned, using his hands to pull me against him. When he started to unbutton my shirt I slapped his hand away and asked what he was doing.

"What does it look like?" he said and laughed. "Look, babe, the windows are tinted. I love you and I know you love me. No more games, Clara. I've waited and paid my dues and now it's time we were together. I know you want to."

He gripped me too tightly on my thigh and licked my earlobe. I pushed him with both hands and looked at him closely. He looked like a wild caged animal. Then I knew. "You're still taking them," I accused in a whisper.

"I have to," he said, not even trying to deny it, "until the meets are done. State is coming up. Then I'll stop. Come on, Clara. Don't be such a stick in the mud. I've been taking them for three months now and you never noticed."

"Well, I notice now." I started to climb out, but he grabbed my arm.

"Where do you think you're going? You can't just leave me hanging like this." He motioned to his boy parts and I felt sick. "Help a guy out, Clara," he sneered and I jerked from him and tried to straighten my clothes as I walked away, leaving my bag and everything.

He yelled at me, where everyone could hear in the parking lot. "Tease! Don't ask for it if you're just not ready for it, honey!" he said snidely and I heard him laugh.

I ran towards the bathroom, feeling tears on my cheeks and everyone's eyes watching me, once again. I rammed right into someone turning the hall corner and felt warm arms go around me. I didn't even care who it was at that point, I just wanted someone, but I knew it was Eli. Without even looking up, I knew it was him.

"What did he do, Clara?" he asked softly.

"He's just being a jerk." I leaned back to look at him as I wiped my eyes and saw that familiar expression, but it seemed tame now. Under control. "I'm sorry I ran into you."

"You didn't. I ran into you." At first I thought he was making a joke, but he meant it. He must have seen what happened and intercepted me. "I'm sorry you had to go through this."

"What do you mean?"

"Nothing. Here." He put his arm around my back and pulled me with him. "Let's get you cleaned up."

He took me to the girls bathroom and I watched fascinated as he came in with me and lifted me so I was sitting on the sink. He looked down and I saw his eyes bulge and his expression turned angry. I looked down and saw two of my shirt buttons were open and the buttons ripped off. Tate had been rougher than I thought.

"Oh," I said and covered myself.

"Here," he said and took his shirt off leaving a black wife beater on. Then he slipped that off, too ,and I heard my breath catch. Oh my, but he was nice looking. He had a huge scar on his chest, over his heart in the shape of a circle. It looked like a brand of some kind but the rest of him distracted me. He was lean yes, but that didn't mean he was missing anything. His arms and upper chest were lumps of muscle and toned skin. His black uniform pants were riding low on his hips, his blue boxers sticking slightly out of the top.

I felt my cheeks burn hot and turned to gaze at the wall, covering my mouth with my fingers.

"Off," he said and motioned with his hand, up.

"What?"

"Shirt, off," he repeated.

"Close your eyes."

He smiled and chuckled silently. "Of course," he conceded.

I unbuttoned my red uniform shirt and as soon as I was done, with his eyes still closed, I felt him tug his wife beater over my head. It smelled heavenly and I bit my lip to keep from sniffing the collar right in front of him. He opened his eyes and pulled my shirt back on over his, doing the buttons so that his shirt peeked out the top and my bra was no longer visible.

"Better?" he asked as he put his shirt back on and wet a paper towel to wipe my face. I assumed my mascara was running.

"Yes, thank you. You're pretty handy."

"Did he hurt you?" He ran a tentative hand down my arm, turning it over to inspect.

"Not really."

He pulled the collar of my shirt down to inspect the bruise and he nodded as I fought to keep my breaths even. "It looks better today."

"Better? When have you seen it?" I asked and watched him closely for some reaction.

The only time he'd seen it was when he came to me when I closed my eyes. He looked up at my eyes now and stared in silent contest...as if daring me to say the words. To say we shared some kind of dream-walk thing. But that was crazy right? I mean, that's just something my subconscious had conjured because I was apparently obsessed with him or something, or maybe my mind made up something to help me get through all this.

"Are you done with him now? Has he hurt you enough to show you he's no good for you?" he said evenly, not answering my question.

"I just...he's got so much going on right now. He wouldn't really hurt me," I protested and looked down as I fingered my popped buttons. "At least , I didn't think so. I don't know what I'm gonna do."

"Look," he said and waited for me to obey. His words were even, but his tone was anything but. "I will not stand by and watch him hurt you again. The next time he does this, I'm going to have to do something about it."

"I don't think they'll be a next time. He just...I-" I took a deep breath and pushed him back a little to hop down. "I'm gonna go. Thank you for helping me. I don't know why you keep coming to my rescue, but I'm grateful," I told him and smiled, walking to the door.

I turned around to look at him. He came around me, so close behind me I could feel his warmth.

"You're more than welcome, Clara Belle," he whispered in my ear and stuck something in my front pocket. "My cell number. Call me if you ever need me."

"How did you know my name?" I asked, but when I turned he was already gone.

~ ~ ~

At lunch I sat with my friends, though I didn't want to, I didn't know what else to do. Tate sat on the end with his boys, looking ripe with guilt. He stared at me across the table, slouched in his chair, and begged me with his eyes to forgive him. I just looked away and refused to look at him again. No one asked if I was ok, not even Sarah. No one asked me why I wasn't sitting with

Tate. They all knew and didn't care or refused to upset the balance of the cool table.

Eli took the only seat available when he showed up, the one Deidre had reserved. She ran her fingers through his hair and kissed his cheek as soon as he sat down.

I waited for him to tell her to stop, something. But no, he just let her touch him. I found myself extremely upset by that. Dee of all people? Sarah was way sweeter if he was looking for someone. But why did he have to be looking? After all the flirting, all the strange chemistry between us... ugh…who was I kidding? I still had a boyfriend. Sort of….

Dee looked right at me a few times, she could tell I was watching, as she sifted his hair or gripped his arm playfully as she spoke into his ear. He looked stoic, but she didn't notice or didn't care. Probably the latter.

After some time, I couldn't just sit there anymore. I got up and went to get a soda from the machine across the room. I realized I shouldn't have after I was halfway across because I was getting lots of sympathy stares and then some ha-she-got-what-she-deserved stares too. It was unnerving. I put my money in the machine and turned to find Patrick.

"Hey, Clara."

"Hey, Pat. What's up?"

"Um...I was wondering...there's a dance coming up." Oh no. Please don't ask me. Patrick was a really tall, cute guy who had an unfortunate case of shy-guy. He hung out with the skateboard crew because they were non-threatening, but I'd always liked him just fine. "I was wondering if you think Sarah would go with me?" he finished.

I smiled. It wasn't me, it was Sarah. Honestly, I knew she would never ever go out with him because he wasn't part of our table. Though, she had once divulged to me that she thought he was adorable. But as I glanced over Pat's shoulder and saw Dee draped all over Eli, I didn't care about that. It might be a good distraction for my group.

"I think you should ask her. Right now. She likes guys who are bold, Pat. Go for it."

"Really? You think so? Ok."

I walked with him back to our table and sat down, turning a quick smile on Dee, then Sarah.

"Sarah, look who came to see you."

Everyone turned to look at Patrick. That's when I felt my first real jolt of guilt. Oh, no. What had I done? I'd practically fed him to the wolves because I was jealous of Dee and Eli. I started to tell Pat never mind, to just forget it, but he'd already started.

"Hey, Sarah."

"Oh?" Dee chimed happily and leaned her back against Eli. "This should be good. Well, go ahead."

"Um...I was just thinking it might be fun to go to the dance together. It's short notice, I know."

"Patrick…um," Sarah stalled. She could be cruel too but not to someone like Pat and not just outright. But apparently, Dee was bent on answering for her.

"You thought she'd go to the dance with you?" Dee shrilled loudly, calling attention from everyone in the lunchroom.

Pat turned a betrayed glance to me before putting them back on her and silently pleading for her to stop.

"I'm sorry I bothered you," he said to Sarah, who sat silently.

"Oh no, we're not finished." Dee stood quickly. "Mike, Tom, get him!"

They grabbed him in on both arms and Dee stood in front of him, smirking like the fake princess she was.

I thought about saying something, but I was already in hot water with the Tate thing and now Eli and you just didn't go up against my friends and make it out unscathed.

"You thought she'd go out with something that looks like I scraped it off my boot?" she sneered and grabbed Sarah's chili bowl from in front of her. I cringed in horror as she handed it to Mike and he dumped it on Patrick's head, right there in the lunch room. Everyone started laughing immediately, taunting. "Now. Go run along and play with the kids at your table. You will never speak to her again, understand?"

He started to fight back, but Mike and Tom were pretty big guys. He probably figured Tate and Eli would join in the fray, too, so he pulled briskly from their grasps.

"Whatever," he grumbled and walked away, leaving chili marks on the floor and wiping his eyes and face with it as the heckles ensued around him.

I covered my mouth to stifle my cry. I wanted to burst into tears for him. No one deserved that, especially not Patrick, and I was the cause. I felt sick.

Then my eyes drifted to Eli and I felt even sicker. He was looking at me with doubt and unbelief. He raised his chin and flicked his eyes towards where Patrick had slinked off to. He was challenging me again. Wanting me to stand up to my friends who were still laughing about 'chili boy'. But I wasn't the one who poured chili on his head was I?

I stood, though I had no intention of intervening. I just stood.

Dee sat back down and when she did, Eli got up. She tried to stop him with a surprised smile, she tried to coax him to sit, having no idea what he was doing.

"Come on, baby. It's not time for bell yet."

He gave her a look that said he knew exactly what time it was.

"I'm not into spoiled princesses who have to stomp on people to feel good about themselves. But thanks anyway," he said smoothly, jerked her arm off of his then walked away. Just like that.

I was as stunned as everyone else as they silently watched him go. The countless times - daily events really - that I'd witnessed of my so called friends torturing other kids could fill a novella. I'd always watched, never stood up to them and never participated but now, as I watched Eli walk away, I realized I may as well have been the one doing it myself; tripping kids, making fun, laughing at, humiliating, pouring chili on their heads, because it was practically the same thing. I stood by and accepted it, was complacent and that may have even been worse.

But Eli was someone to respect and be proud of...unlike me.

I grabbed my bag and went to go, too, but Sarah grabbed my arm.

"What are you doing?"

"I'm done," I said.

"Where are you going, Clara?" Dee asked even though Sarah just had.

"I'm done," I said harder. Her face froze in a mask of hatefulness.

"Oh," Mike chanted moving behind me and slapped my ponytail to mock me. "Look who's all high and mighty now."

Without another word, I turned and left. I heard Tate telling Mike not to touch me, but I kept going. When I reached the hall, I saw Eli heading into our class. He looked back at me and watched me for a second before going in.

The bell rang and I looked for Patrick to apologize but didn't find him. I felt wretched. I heard my name behind me. Tate. I bolted the other way. Math class was fast paced as she did lots of board work for us and since I didn't sit next to Eli, I didn't get to talk to him. When I got to Art, Eli was there already and he didn't say a word as I sat down.

"Hey, you ok?" I asked.

"Oh, I'm fine," he said softly and looked at me. "My conscience is clean. How's yours?"

I felt all my breath leave me. He turned to face the class and didn't look back at me again. I felt horrible. Not only was I guilty over Patrick, but now Eli thought I was a bad person. He knew I was just as guilty as the rest of them, but called me on it. That stung worse than the guilt.

When the bell rang he shot out of his seat and hurried out the door. I wanted to go to the bathroom and cry but didn't. Somehow I trudged my way to the hall and out the school doors.

Four

There was a pep rally and bonfire that night so I had to be at the school even though I so did not want to be. I met Sarah at the table but she was too hyped and I wasn't in the mood for her banter. I stood on the other side with a couple of t-shirts in hand and tried to smile normally.

I saw Patrick and his friends coming in the door. I wondered why they even bothered to come to these things. It wasn't like they were all about school spirit or anything. I watched him as he laughed and pushed and joked with his friends. He saw me watching and his smile disappeared into a frown. He looked away immediately and hurried inside. I felt like the worst kind of person. But at least he came; he showed everyone he wasn't going to hide and cower just because they embarrassed him. I felt someone behind me and turned to tell Sarah to please just leave me by myself for a minute. But it was Eli.

"Eli," I breathed.

"Clara," he said gruffly. "I see Patrick's here. Can't keep a nice guy down, huh?"

"I guess not. I'm glad he came," I told him but couldn't lift my face to look at him.

"Why? Dee and Mike not finished with him yet," he said snidely.

"No, it's not that," I said softly and couldn't find anything else to say.

I just stared up at him and wondered if there was any way to fix all the mess. He grabbed my arm gently and pulled me to the wall. He leaned me against it with a hand pushing my stomach and though his words were harsh, his face was pleading.

"You are so much better than them; than this. You're not the kind person who hurts people. I know you're not. You choose your own actions. No one can make you do something, Clara."

"I know that," I said and pushed his hand away. "I didn't mean for that to happen to him. I didn't do it on purpose."

"But you don't ever stand up to them. They make their whole life about ruining others. The Clara I thought I was getting to know, who's sweet and sad and thoughtful all at the same time, wouldn't be ok with other people being hurt like that."

He was right and I was so done with it all, everything; the guilt, the sadness, the need for things to be perfect and normal. I pushed him aside so I could leave and I went straight home. Sarah yelled at me to come back, that we weren't done yet, but I didn't care and didn't stop. And she didn't call me to check on me that night either.

Mrs. Ruth caught me in the hall, wiping her hands on a dishtowel of something she was cooking for dinner.

"Clara, I thought you had a match tonight?"

"I did but I left. I'm gonna go to bed, I'm not feeling too well."

"Are you ok?" she touched my forehead with the backs of her fingers. "You don't feel warm but you looked a little flushed."

"I'm fine. I'm not really hungry, just gonna go to bed. Don't worry. I'm just tired," I included so she wouldn't feel the need to check up on me.

She called up to me with a sweet "Feel better".

After a shower in which I cried in self pity and stayed way too long in the hot water, I sat on my bed and debated shutting my eyes. I mean it wasn't real. Apparently I was having some kind of breakdown. The death of my parents had pushed me over the edge somehow but it was only now that I was feeling the effects; a delayed response due to denial or shock maybe. I didn't know, but I did know that I wasn't ready to see Eli when I closed my eyes. To see his disappointment in me and hear him tell me I was stupid for worrying about Tate and everything else.

But I knew I couldn't fight it all night. So I lay back and closed my eyes and was met with nothing but darkness. Eventually I drifted to sleep and Eli never made an appearance. I guessed I was going crazy after all.

~ ~ ~

I decided to lie.

I was in no mood to face everyone at school, with their smug grins that had no place on their faces. I didn't want to face Tate and his guilt and dodge the begging ceremony I knew he was trying to stage. And I didn't want to face Eli.

So, I lied.

I told Mrs. Ruth that I was sick and threw together a concoction that resembled what I was going for into the toilet. She took barely a peak and turned green, yelling that I was excused from school as she practically ran down the hall. I felt bad for lying but strangely also wanted to giggle at how easy it had been. I hardly ever missed school.

All that day I stayed in bed and watched vamp show reruns. I sulked and tried to not think about Tate or Eli. I was basically a coward but I knew I couldn't be one all day. There was a match at school that night and I had to attend, especially after running out on last night.

In the afternoon, I got up and took another shower. Mrs. Ruth had tapped on my door several times to check on me but I just assured her I was fine until she went away. Now I could hide no longer. My life awaited me and I had to face it.

So I grabbed a biscuit off the stove on my way out and waved to the babies, telling Mrs. Ruth I just needed rest because I felt fine. She didn't look convinced but, didn't stop me. Pastor Paul caught me at the door and hugged me, kissing my forehead. It reminded me so much of my father that I had to stop the gasp that always wanted to seep out. I squeezed my eyes tight to stop the wetness and looked up to him with a smile.

He must have seen it written all over my face. His expression softened even more, which didn't seem possible. There was understanding there, not sympathy.

"Your parents would be so proud of you, Clara. I just wanted to tell you that."

"Thanks," I croaked and turned away. I highly doubted that they'd be proud of me today. "I have to get to the school. See you later."

"Bye, honey. Midnight."

"I remember," I called over my shoulder and waved without turning.

Then I felt my pocket buzz with a text message right as I reached the parking lot to the gym.

Meet me outside the away locker room after the match. I want to talk. Please. Just for a minute. – Tate

I knew I should have just disregarded it but I had to talk to him eventually. I decided I'd go and tell him I needed some time to think. He needed to get himself together as well. It would be better by ourselves instead of talking at school in front of everybody.

I went to the booth and got right to work selling tickets and merchandise. Another girl, Tamara, was helping today but I didn't say anything to her or anyone else.

Once it was time for the match I made my way inside. For some reason I found myself searching the stands for Patrick. I saw him at the bottom bleacher with his friends but there was someone else who had stopped to talk to him…Eli. They were chatting and laughing and I was too ashamed to face Eli or Patrick right then, so I went to turn, but Eli saw me at the last second. His violet gaze pierced me to my spot and I stared back at him. Finally he released me and I almost stumbled away. I went to the side where I never sat for the games. I just couldn't deal with anyone right then.

A few of the people sitting there gave me a funny look but ultimately left me alone. Everyone knew who I was and where I sat. I hadn't realized how shallow and predictable I had become.

The match went on without a hitch. I watched as Sarah looked around for me but finally decided to just ogle the opposing team. Tate looked for me too but didn't see me. He looked disappointed.

We won though and at the end of the match, I got up to leave. I saw Eli making his way to me. Once again I wasn't ready to hear more of his disappointment in me or lectures so I turned and hurried out the door. I made my way to the guest shower housing. I walked slowly, giving them time to be packed up. I heard talking and figured Tate was there with some of the guys or something but when I turned the corner, I saw that he wasn't talking at all.

He had Deidre pushed up against the side of the building and was kissing her. His hand drifted up her skirt to places I didn't want to think about. She opened her eyes and when she saw me. She pulled back and smiled.

"Baby, what if someone catches us?" she asked him sweetly.

"We won't get caught," he murmured against her lips and hoisted her skirt higher. "That's why we always do this here, because no one else ever comes over here. Now, be quiet and-"

I gasped and covered my mouth in disgust. He heard. He dropped her and turned to me shocked.

"What the hell are you doing way over here, Clara?" he asked and tried to straighten his clothes.

"You texted me," I said incredulously. "Why would you text me so I would find you like this?"

"I didn't text you. Clara..." he started, but I backed away.

"Oh, Tate, here you go. You left this in my car...earlier," Dee said happily and twiddled his phone in her fingers before giving it to him.

"You?" he asked and it all fell into place. "You texted her so she'd find us? Why?"

"Because I'm tired of being your little secret. If she won't give it up for you, fine, date me instead and solve that problem, but you can't have it both ways." She looked at me and smiled her best winning smile. "I got him after all didn't I?"

Tate turned to look at me. He was angry and upset and sorry all at the same time. And none of it mattered.

"Clara, please...I never meant to hurt you, I just...I needed some...release with all the stress in my life and you weren't there for me in that way so I just... This hasn't been going on that long, just the past couple weeks," he stammered and ran his hands through his hair, like he knew it was hopeless. "It meant nothing," he told me in a groan and Dee huffed.

"You can't justify what you did," I argued. "If we ever had a chance of getting back together, that's gone now."

"Clara, no. Please! Babe, I'm begging you," he called, but I took off running towards the parking lot. "Stop! Wait!"

Angry tears dripped down my face. All this time they'd both been going behind my back. Dee was getting back at me and Tate was using her and she didn't even care as long as I suffered for it.

I wiped my face as the last of the people climbed into their cars. I saw Patrick getting into his old yellow VW bug with his friends and he saw me. He stopped the door in mid swing as he opened it and peered at me, clearly seeing me crying. I sniffled and turned to make my way to the street. One quick look back showed he'd made the decision to just go and not worry about me.

As I reached the sidewalk and stopped for traffic, I felt someone behind me. I could tell it was Eli. I wasn't sure how I always knew but I did, without a doubt.

"You were right about Tate," I said without turning and tried to ease the strain from my words. "He had no intentions of not hurting me anymore. Tate and Dee have been making a fool out of me. I got what I deserved. I hope you're happy."

I started to cross the four lane, but he pulled me to a stop with a hand on my arm. "Now why would I be happy about that?"

I refused to look at him. I stared down at the black Chuck Taylors he was wearing.

"Because I'm a horrible person. I'm a brat, a tease, a sheep. I'm a bad person who lets bad things happen. You said so yourself." I tried to cross the street again, but he stopped me once more with a grasp to my fingers. I huffed and turned to look at him, my voice raising to a yell. "What! What do you want? I can't handle anymore lectures tonight, ok. I can't handle anymore disappointment. Just leave me alone," I finished softly and tried one last time to leave his grasp, but this time when he pulled me back, he pulled me to him.

I felt the warmth of his chest and it felt so much like I belonged there; like it was home. He lifted my chin with his finger, his forearm around my back, and looked at me intensely. "You are not a bad person and you don't deserve this."

"Yes, I do!" I sniffed and felt more tears glide down to my jaw.

He wiped one away with his thumb. "You're better than them, Clara. You don't have to follow them just because that's what you've always done. Sometimes, you have to make up your own mind about what's right."

"I don't know what I'm doing anymore. I don't even...belong here anymore."

"Because Tate cheated on you? He doesn't define you, Clara."

"It's not just Tate. It's everything. I'm only involved in Spirit Squad because my mom wanted me to be. My dad was ecstatic I was dating Tate; the wrestling star and the Mayor's son. I felt obligated to my parents to continue to be who I was when they were alive. But I'm not happy," I cried harder.

"You have to make your own happy. You can't depend on other people for that."

"Are you happy?" I asked softly, looking up at him.

He looked at me closely, watching me watch him. Then he bent his head and kissed me, softly and gently at first. I was completely confused and enthralled by how much I'd wanted him to do that and I wound my arms around his middle as our lips met for the first time in agonizing weeks. Then I opened my mouth to his out of sheer requirement.

He had a tongue ring that I had no prior knowledge of and my blood heated to think about it as it clanked gently once against my teeth. His fingers on my chin moved to my cheek and then to my hair. It sent thrills through me and I shivered and pressed myself closer. He groaned, a strained sound, and pulled away.

We stood close, our foreheads touching and our hot breaths mingling and swirling, making me feel intoxicated in the foggy dark parking lot. He pulled back to look at me and smiled a little bit. Then kissed me once more softly on the lips.

"I've wanted to do that ever since I saw you in the park that day." He pulled my hand up to kiss my palm then looked both ways and pulled me across the street. "Go straight inside," he told me as he pushed me towards my porch.

Then he walked away and took off down the street towards his house. I was in stunned awe. I walked in a daze up the hall and wondered what had caused him to end our kiss so abruptly. I also wondered why I wasn't more upset about Dee and Tate. I was, but I would think I'd be in hysterics; I should've been. But I wasn't in agony. I was hurt, but I was more angry at the betrayal. I had no idea what tomorrow was going to bring, but I knew there was no way I could just sit with them at lunch and pretend that what they did was all ok anymore. And even if Eli hadn't just kissed me, Tate and I would still be *so* over.

Things were about to change.

Pastor and Mrs. Ruth were watching television and the children were already in bed so I crept down the hall quietly so as not to disturb them and went straight to my dresser. I had some soul cleaning-out to do.

The prom picture from last year - trashed it. The picture of the whole gang at a beach party this summer, all wearing our bathing suits and jumping into the air - gone. The photo booth pics Tate insisted we get together at the mall where he kissed me in a different spot in every one - done with them. The ribbons I saved from Middle School Cheer camp from Sarah and my pompoms – through with them. The movie stubs and Grad Nite ticket I saved from the past years – down it floated into the pile that was my life. Everything I thought was important was no longer.

I threw on my sleep clothes, a long Navy t-shirt of my sisters that she gave me when she left. Essentially, it was a guilt gift. I paused and brought Eli's shirt that I'd just taken off to my nose. It still smelled just like him and I held back the need to groan about it. I slipped under the covers, his shirt in between my fingers, and was already dreading school tomorrow. But right then, I was ready to close my eyes. Ready to see if Eli would still be there in the dark of my eyelids, waiting for me.

~ ~ ~

I was in the school parking lot. I had on my long t-shirt and nothing else and I looked around, but I was alone. I leaned against a car that had been left in the lot and for a second wondered if I had sleep walked over here and this was real, not what happened when I closed my eyes. Then I felt him. I turned my head to see him making his way to me. I wondered if things would be different between us now. He'd never kissed me in the dream-walk things before.

He answered me almost immediately.

He pulled me to him and pressed his lips to mine hungrily. I pulled him, too, so he'd lean with me against the car and he came willingly as he continued to kiss all the good sense out of me. Once again he pulled away too soon, it seemed, once I got worked up.

"I'm glad you came," I said breathlessly.

"I couldn't not come," he answered. Then he lifted me to sit on the hood of the car as he came to stand between my knees. "You're laying with my shirt," he said knowingly and smirked.

"How do you know that?" I asked seriously.

"I know lots of things," he said cryptically.

"Please, Eli. I am so confused. Is this real? Are you really here or am I just wishful thinking every night? How is this even possible?"

"I don't want to mess things up, Clara," he whispered and ran a hand absently down my arm.

"You won't. I just want to know."

He looked around, blowing an exasperated breath. "Walk with me?"

"Are you going to answer my question?"

"Will it matter as to whether you walk with me or not?"

I huffed, but smiled at him. "You're impossible." I let him help me down and he took my hand. I felt completely comfortable, even though I was only in a long t-shirt. "Where are we going?"

"I thought I'd show you the park at night. It's pretty amazing."

"You hang out at the park at night?"

"Sometimes. I'm supposed to be...there's things I'm supposed to be doing, but I...I can't anymore. So after I visit you, I go there," he confessed.

"Eli, please," I pulled him to stop in the middle of the streetlamp lit road. "You have to tell me what's going on. Are you in some kinda trouble or something?"

"Sweet, Clara," he said softly and touched my cheek, rubbing caresses with his thumb. "Are you going to save me if I am?"

"I'll do anything I can," I said and looked him right in the eye.

"There's nothing you can do I'm afraid. But I love it that you'd try anyway," he said and kissed me again, lingering.

Then he towed me to the swings, setting me in one and pushing me in a slow easy rhythm. We stayed there for a long time just like that, just being with each other. Sometimes we talked about school or things we liked but, mostly we just enjoyed each other's space and time. I realized he was not going to answer my questions but I didn't want to push. We lay in the grass and looked at the bugs buzzing and humming around the streetlamps for hours it seemed. At the end of our time, he walked me home.

"If this is a dream or something, why does it matter where we end up? I'm still in my bed, aren't I?"

"Yes, but I wouldn't want you to think I wasn't a gentleman. Besides, I've been dying to kiss you every time I drop you off on your doorstep." I blushed and he smiled wider as he leaned in, pulling me up to meet his lips. It was easy and controlled. Then he leaned back and touched my bottom lip with his thumb. "By the way, what we're doing is called a Reverie. It's not a dream, because you're still awake. That's why I need to leave, so you can get some sleep. Goodnight. I'll see you tomorrow, CB."

I could only nod and touch my lips in wonder. Had it all been real? I felt a little insane, but giddy, too. It was official; I was crazy obsessed. I giggled as I made my way back to my room and saw myself laying there in the bed. That scene and the shock jolted me aware and I sat up in bed quickly, back in myself.

I lay back down and smiled as I wondered if it had been real at all. It was crazy to think so, but I wanted it to be so badly.

~ ~ ~

By the time I reached school the next morning, my heart was in a tizzy. I was scared; scared of what I was going to do with Tate and Dee and all the rest of them. I was a little early this morning so I sat in the courtyard under the oak with a bench around it, along with everyone else in their little groups but, I was alone.

A couple of smiley freshman came up and asked me about joining the spirit squad. I was debating quitting, though I didn't tell them that, so I directed them to Sarah. They gave me funny looks when I pointed them her way. I knew it was because I wasn't sitting with my friends. I just smiled extra brightly and waited for them to move on.

I was about to pull out my math book when I heard a commotion and looked to see Dee, Mike and Megan chanting 'chili boy' across the yard. Patrick was about ten feet from them and had just sat down with his friends. He shook his head and looked away from them angrily but they didn't stop. Chili boy? That wasn't even a good insult!

My mind made itself up right then and before I even realized what I was doing, I'd packed up my stuff and was making my way to Patrick.

Dee and Mike looked deviously gleeful as they slapped hands. Dee watched me giddily as she actually thought that even after her betrayal – something that was so hurtful and evil that I was confused as to how she was really even a human girl – I was coming to sit with them, but when I veered off her smile turned to disbelief.

I heard Mike mutter, "What is she doing?"

"Clara!" she called and waved for me to come. "I forgive you. Come sit with us," she said snidely with a little evil smile.

"Yeah!" Mike yelled, too, even though he had no idea what was going on. "It's all good, baby."

I glared at them as I made my way to Patrick. When she realized what I was doing she turned bright red. No one crossed my group. They were like the Mob of high school.

"Patrick," I said softly and saw him stiffen before he turned. He looked at me with a little frown and waited for me to say something else. "I'm sorry. I didn't know...I didn't mean to put you in the middle of all that. I'm really sorry, and they were wrong to act like that."

"You were sitting right there with them, as I recall," he said smoothly, but I could tell he was fighting for control.

"Yes, I was," I said and heard my voice choke back tears, "and I'm ashamed about that. I just wanted to say I was sorry," I repeated and walked away towards the school.

He watched me and when he saw me pass Dee and the rest of them, he yelled my name. I turned to see him standing, his friends looking between the two of us. He waved me back and I started slowly his way again. I could see Mike and Dee and the others watching us. I could practically feel the anger pouring off them as they glared daggers. And Dee. She thought she had me, that I'd have to just suck it up and endure her and everything she'd done to me. That I'd just take it, but she was wrong and now she was mad.

"Clara, get your butt over here, or have you not gotten his notes yet," she yelled and laughed.

Mike snickered as he bumped fist with Tommy when he walked up to join them. Megan and Sarah were just as happy as the rest of them as they giggled into their fists.

I joined Patrick, my books in my hands, my bag over my shoulder. I looked up to him tentatively.

"What'd you do?" he asked, his arms folded over his chest.

"What?"

"What did you do to the ice patrol to get shunned?"

"I didn't do anything. I just found out who my real friends were."

"And who are they?" he asked and cocked his head.

"I don't have any," I said in a cheerful voice with a big fake smile.

They all burst out laughing.

"You're all right, kid," Patrick said and put his arm around my shoulder. "Come on, sit with us."

I sat down and really got a look of Patrick's friends. There were five of them that hung out regularly, four guys and one girl, but the girl had an almost shaved head and a nose ring connected to her earring so I was intimidated and kept my mouth shut with her. Patrick introduced me to everyone and I felt bad because they all knew who I was, but I didn't know any of their names except Patrick.

Then I felt it; the awareness that Eli was there. I looked up to see him staring at me. He smiled wide and knowingly. When he started to make his way to us, Dee bolted from my old group and wrapped her arms around his neck. He pulled her off gently and set her aside as he continued to walk to us.

She huffed and started to follow him, but saw where he was going and slowed. He walked right up to me, pulled me up from my bench and kissed me right there in front of everyone. I heard Patrick and his friends whistling and clapping before Eli released me, my cheeks blazing a hot crimson. I saw Dee walk red faced and angry to grab her purse and then Megan and Sarah following her as she stalked away.

He leaned down to whisper in my ear, "I'm so proud of you, CB." I just smiled up at him. Then he spoke again. "I told you I'd see you tomorrow, didn't I?"

I gasped and grabbed his shirt front. In the Reverie, he'd said that. It was real? "Tell me, please," I pleaded.

"We'll talk later," he said with a smile. "At my place."

"Promise?"

"I promise."

"Hey, Eli. What's up, man?" Patrick said and they bumped fist and did some strange hand shake, arm bumping thing. It looked intricate. "Dude, we've gotta show you the town this week, man. There's a club here that's pretty sick, if you go on the right night."

"Yeah, sounds good."

"Cool." The bell rang ending any further comments. "See you guys later."

Eli walked me to homeroom, brushing my shoulder with his and we got many looks, but I no longer cared. Everyone was used to seeing me with Tate and I'm sure it was strange for them to see me with Eli all of a sudden, but I could care less. Eli was smiling sexily as we walked and when we reached my homeroom door he leaned in, forcing me to retreat to the wall.

"I'm so glad I can do this now," he confessed softly and rubbed my arm discreetly.

"Me, too." I groaned, tugging on his shirt front, my actions refuting my next words, "I've gotta go."

"I'll see you at lunch, ok?" he said through a broad grin that displayed his enjoyment of my actions.

"Ok," I said and bit my lip.

I looked both ways and pulled him to me, feeling his smile against my skin as I kissed his cheek. But a loud bang startled us apart. We both looked over to see Tate standing at my locker, his fist firmly planted into an imprint in the metal where he had punched. He was looking at us - glaring was a more appropriate description.

He pushed off and turned with everyone watching him like he was a ticking time bomb. He punched another locker on his way and then disappeared out of sight.

"Crap," I muttered.

"Hey. Don't worry about him," Eli said softly and tucked my hair behind my ear. "I'll take care of him if he wants trouble."

"He's still using."

"I know."

I sighed. "Ok. See you at lunch. Be careful, ok?"

He smirked. "You're cute when you worry."

"Ha, ha," I said and smiled before heading into class.

~ ~ ~

"I can't believe you," Sarah scoffed and banged her locker shut as she started down the hall. "I mean, you already had this amazing hot guy and now you take the other available hot guy. What's with you? I don't remember you being this selfish," Sarah said hotly.

"Sarah, Tate hit me. He cheated on me. He's using steroids. What was I supposed to do? Pretend it didn't happen just to keep the clique happy? Eli has been there for me through all this."

"How convenient," she said and tried to go around me but I stopped her.

"Sarah, don't be like this. You weren't mad at Dee for hanging all over him, so why are you mad at me?"

"It's different."

"Why?" I asked in bewilderment.

"Because she's Dee and you're you. I don't know it's just different. I didn't expect him to go for her anyway."

"I can't help it if he likes me. I didn't chase him, it just worked out this way," I explained.

"It just worked out this way," she repeated blandly and stopped to look at me. "And what was that stunt with Patrick this morning. WTH, Clara?"

"What they were doing was wrong and you know it. Dee and Mike and everybody else shouldn't be able to just do whatever they want to people just because they are who they are."

"Whatever. You never complained before."

"I know. And I'm making up for lost time now."

"You're not going to sit with us at lunch, are you?"

I hesitated, already knowing the answer but dreading her reaction.

"No. I can't. I don't want to be around Tate."

"Well, I guess that's it then, isn't it?" she spouted and started walking again.

"Is it really that important to you? To be sitting at that table?"

"Yes! It's all I have, Clara! I'm not pretty like you. I don't have guys throwing themselves at me. All I have are them and that table."

I stopped following her and let her go. "You can sit with me anytime you want," I called after her.

I met Eli at the door to our next class. I'd told him I wanted to talk to Sarah before class. He had wanted to go with me because of Tate but I assured him his class was way away from ours.

"How'd it go?" he asked and ushered me into class with a hand on my back.

"As expected."

"Sorry."

"It's ok. If paying for your past sins were easy, everyone would do it right?"

He smirked down at me.

"Very philosophical. And true."

"Seats, people," the teacher grunted as she entered and I made my way to mine.

Class went by slowly, waiting for lunch. I dreaded it but, also welcomed it. I needed to get this over with and the sooner the better. I wondered if Patrick would have a problem with my sitting with them or not. I was sure Eli and I could sit alone somewhere else.

I laughed under my breath. I was an outcast! It was hilarious and liberating. After spending my whole life being seen as some spoiled and undeserving privileged cool kid, I was a loser! And it felt awesome. I turned to Eli to see him smiling at me, like he knew what I was thinking. I smiled back and bit my lip when he winked at me. I heard a loud 'ahem' from the front of the room and looked to see the teacher with a brow raised, eyeing us both.

I mouthed a sorry and she shook her head in amusement before going on with class. Then the bell rang.

Eli and I walked together after we went to his locker. I realized that was why he always got there after us. We shuffled our way to the cafeteria and stopped in the doorway, my heart galloping. Eli took my cold hand in his and brought it up to his mouth to kiss my fingers. He leaned towards me and whispered in my ear.

"It's ok, Clara Belle. I'm right here with you."

Five

"How do you know my name?"

"I'll explain it all tonight. Promise."

"Is your family going to be there?" I said, feeling suddenly way more anxious about that than I felt for this cafeteria right now.

"No. I live alone."

"Live alone? At eighteen? But I thought you said you live with your parents?"

"Sweetheart," he crooned and my heart jumped. No one had ever called me that before and it did funny things to me. I bit my lip. He groaned and pressed his face to my hair. "Clara, you're killing me," he whispered.

"What do you mean?" I whispered, confused.

"Nothing." He took a deep breath. "I'll tell you everything. I'll answer every question...tonight. Ok?"

"Ok."

"But promise me something."

"Alright."

He hesitated and looked at me seriously and for long seconds.

"Promise you won't hate me."

He'd said that in a Reverie once too.

"Why would I hate you? Eli, you're scaring me. What, do you have a wife and kids somewhere?" I joked and he laughed sadly and pushed my hair back from my face.

"I only wish it was that simple. Don't worry, it's nothing like that. I have faith that you'll be able to handle it...I just can't lose you. Not after only just finding you."

"I have no idea what that means, but I promise to keep an open mind."

"That's all I can ask of you," he said and took my bag from my shoulder. I followed him as he set our stuff at a table and then pushed me from behind with his hands on my sides to get in line. "I'm starving."

"Me too. What are you getting?"

"Hmmm. So many choices," he mused sarcastically.

I looked it all over. The lunch lady, who'd I'd never met before because I never ate school food, gave me a foul look as I left a gap between me and the guy in front of me in my indecision.

"I'll take the chicken fingers. Please."

She slopped them on my plate and I trudged down the line, after grabbing a juice and honey mustard sauce. Then I remembered that I had no idea what lunch cost and I had no money on me. Eli skipped me at the register and said he was paying for both. He smirked at me and we made our way to the table. Tate was already seated with everyone else and they stared at me in disbelief. Tate's face was tight, his fist balled up on the table and he stared me down all the way until I sat down. Dee looked like she was about to explode but then made her way over to Tate. She rubbed his shoulder but he threw her hand off and glared at her before looking back at me.

I sat with my back to them and looked at Patrick tentatively to see if he'd object to my sitting with them. He saw me looking and winked. I smiled and tasted my chicken. It was pretty good and tasted nothing like the feet everyone claimed. All the guys talked about this club they'd been to the night before. Monoxide. It was supposed to be an everything club, different nights for different tastes. Like Monday was chick rock night, Tuesday was Goth and Pain night (I didn't ask him to further that explanation) and Thursday nights were rock night and they had live bands there.

Today was Wednesday so naturally they asked if we wanted to go with them tomorrow night. Apparently it was a weekly ritual for them. Eli looked at me and shrugged but then his expression changed and he cleared his throat.

"We'll let you know tomorrow," he said carefully and I realized he thought there might not be a tomorrow for him and me.

He was worried about whatever it was he was going to tell me; that I'd want nothing to do with him. That frightened me a little but I knew it was possible for him to go into my subconscious. I was already believing and open minded to the supernatural at this point. What was he going to say? He was an angel or something?

When the bell rang I turned to see Tate already gone. Good. Eli walked me to class and later in Art, we had to do a sketch portrait of our desk partner.

"Oh, I can't wait to see this," Eli snickered as he posed, his head on his hand, looking at me.

"Don't move. That's perfect," I said with a hand up.

I started on his hair and outlined his face. His nose and lips were next. I lingered on his mouth, getting the shape of his smirk just right. His eyes and his eyebrow ring. His ears and neck. His arm holding up his jaw, lean but muscular and sinewy. The bell dinged to tell us it was time to switch.

"Can I see it?"

"Sure," I slid it towards him, "but it's not that good."

He pulled it to him and looked at it. His smile was genuine, I could tell, as he glanced between me and the drawing.

"It's really good, CB."

"CB?" I asked, amused.

"CB for Clara Belle," he said and smirked. "I didn't know you could draw like this."

"I can't draw. That's just playing around."

"Yes, you can, I'm looking at it."

"Whatev. How do you want me?" He raised his eyebrow at that I felt my cheeks heat. "You know what I mean."

He cocked his head looking at me and thinking.

"Ok. How about you turn away from me and look over your shoulder." He took my shoulder and turned me on my stool, then pulled my face to look over my shoulder at him. "Just like that."

He immediately reached for his pencil, without looking away from me, and started to draw. He'd focus on me and then back on his paper. He squinted and furrowed his brow in concentration. It was adorable. After less time than it took me, he was done. He didn't wait for me to ask to see it, he just pushed it in front of me.

It was beautiful. The edges were faded and smeared looking and then clear and focused in the middle. Especially my eyes. He made them darker and bolder lines than anything else to make them stand out. I was in complete awe. I looked up to see him watching me.

"Eli, oh my gosh," I gushed.

"I've had a lot of years to perfect it," he said softly and rubbed a finger over the cheek of my picture.

"Eighteen?" I said in jest.

He just smiled and put a hand on mine, rubbing my knuckles with his thumb...and studiously avoided my question. I gave him a look that told him I knew exactly what he was doing and he chuckled silently.

"Ok, class. Now I want you to all display your work on the wall. Just hang your portraits from the clothes pins and after a week of viewing you can take them home. Now before the bell-" The bell rang. "Wait! I want you to all bring in something you do overnight. Anything you want to do and we'll discuss the different types of art, drawings, painting, and brush strokes tomorrow."

I got up slowly, waiting for Eli. I wondered if I was going to his house right then or if he wanted to wait until later. He took my bag from me once again and led me from the room and down the hall to the door, then through the parking lot to the road. I noticed how he knew just where to go where we'd miss Tate's truck in the lot.

"Do you need to let them," he motioned towards my house, "know you're going to my house?"

"Yeah, I do." I looked at him. "Come with me."

"Are you sure? They won't mind me just coming unannounced?"

"No. He's a Pastor," I laughed. "We have people in and out all the time."

"Alright.

We walked across the street and I called out when I opened the door.

"Hey, I'm home."

"Clawa!" I heard and then the patter of swift, small feet.

"Hey." I snatched her up and hoisted her to my hip to keep my balance. "Hannah, hey, this is my friend, Eli."

"Hi, Ewi," she chimed. So frigging cute. Eli laughed too.

"Well, hello there," he said and reached his hand out to shake hers. She took it and as he shook it gently and when he smiled she turned bashful and buried her grin in my neck. "Aww. Did I make you blush?" he crooned and smiled at me.

"And this is Josiah," I said as I felt a small hand tugging the hem of my shirt back.

"Hey," Jo said.

"Hey, sport," Eli said and held his hand out for a low five. Josiah slapped it eagerly and grinned. "How are you, man?"

"I'm good. How are you? Man," Josiah said awkwardly, trying to play big boy.

"I'm awesome," Eli chuckled.

"Where's your mom, Jo?" I asked and followed his point to the kitchen. "Mrs. Ruth, hey. This is Eli, the guy I told you about."

"You talked about me, huh?" Eli whispered in my ear behind me before making his way around and smiling as he said 'Hi' to Mrs. Ruth.

"Hi there, young man. It's nice to meet you."

"Nice to meet you, too."

"Are you staying for supper?"

"Actually, I wanted to ask if you minded if I took Clara out for dinner. And then go back to my house for a little while?"

"And where do you live, Eli?"

"A couple streets over. At the bed and breakfast."

"Oh, I love that house! Are your parents renovating it?"

"Sort of," Eli answered and quickly changed the subject. "So I can ask your husband for permission to take out Clara if I need to," he said respectfully.

"Oh, he's at the church tonight. He hosts the AA meetings so he won't be home. But if you'll write your cell phone number on the fridge right there on that pad, them I'm perfectly fine with Clara going with you, if you bring her home by midnight."

"Yes, ma'am," he said smiling and went to do what she asked.

I debated going to change my clothes but didn't want Eli to think I was more shallow than he already did, so I just said goodbye to Mrs. Ruth and we were gone. We walked to his house, the street was loud and noisy from school traffic, and he opened the passenger door to a black '69 Chevy Chevelle in front of his house.

"This is your car?" I stopped in awe.

"Yep."

"Why don't you drive it to school?"

"Because I can walk, it's so close. Plus," he swept his arm for me to enter, "I don't want to answer questions about how an eighteen year old kid can afford a car like this."

"I see," I said, though I really didn't, as I climbed in and he shut my door.

Once he jumped in his side and started the deep rumbling engine, he pulled out and started down the street the opposite way.

"So I'm assuming this is a classic or something?' His face was quite funny when he looked at me, like I was a totally clueless girly girl, so I forged on. "Where are we going?"

"Do you like pizza?"

"Sure, who doesn't?" I said laughing. "What kind of question is that to ask a teenager?"

"The times have changed."

"You are very cryptic, Eli."

"I know," he muttered through a chuckle. "I'm sorry."

"You can't tell me what's going on first and then take me to eat?"

"No. I want you to enjoy your meal."

"Eli, please," I said, turning to him. "You're really freaking me out-"

"Hey, hey," he said sweetly and reached for my hand. "I promised didn't I? I will tell you everything, but you can't be scared. Ok? I know I haven't earned your trust but I need you to trust me for tonight."

"Eli, really, this is..." I sighed.

"I know. Please, Clara? Please trust me."

I sighed again and said nothing, just looked out the window. It was strange how I felt so at ease with him but I didn't really know him. Something was definitely happening. I mean the Reveries...they were real. It was real. I was confused about a lot of things but the fact that he didn't just walk into my life by accident was evident to me. So I sat and waited and tried to be patient.

We arrived at the pizza place and he came around to open my door. I took his offered hand and let him pull me up but after he shut the door he stopped. He looked at me and his face almost looked regretful as he pushed my hair back from my face. He leaned closer, putting his hands on the car on either side of me, and hovered there, just beyond my lips. His eyes pleaded with me. He was waiting for me…to inch forward and meet him, to say I understood even though there was no reason for me to trust him.

I lifted up on my toes and bunched his shirt front to steady myself as I pressed my lips to his. He hesitated at first, waiting to see if I was just humoring him or if I was for real. After feeling his warm lips on mine, I was definitely for real. I felt too warm all of a sudden and opened my mouth under his. That was what he was waiting for and he leaned against me, kissing me deeper. I felt his small groan as his hand moved to my cheek and my pulse banged behind my ribs. My breaths were practically non-existent by this point.

I pushed him gently away to catch my breath and his lips released me but barely. I could feel his breath on my face as he pressed his forehead to mine.

"Clara." He released a ragged sigh. "You're too much," he groaned.

"What?" I whispered.

"You're just so..." He shook his head. "You're everything that I..." He sighed harshly and leaned away from me, holding his hand out to me. "Come on. Let me buy you a pizza."

I went willingly and followed him to a table. He ordered us a large pineapple and ham because I told him that was my favorite.

"So...you don't have any other family other than a sister?" he asked.

"Well, I have a couple uncles. Why?"

"I just wondered why you lived with the Pastor and his family instead of your own family."

"Well, for one thing I didn't want to change schools my senior year but also, neither of my uncles wanted to live with a teenage girl so...the Pastor came and asked if I wanted to stay with them until I graduated. So they are my foster family I guess."

"They seem nice."

"They are," I agreed and swirled the ice in my cola. "They're really great."

"What are you going to do after school?"

"No idea. You?"

"Depends on some things," he said vaguely.

"What things?"

"Are you gonna eat that?" he asked and grabbed the rest of my second piece, taking a big bite of it.

"You are such an avoider," I accused and he laughed. "I don't get it. You won't tell me anything? Why?"

"I don't want to scare you yet with that answer."

"Ok. Well let's go then because I'm so very ready to understand what's going on with you."

"Ok."

I heard the excitement and the reluctance in his voice. I followed him to the car and he drove to his house. It was a huge blue house that had been vacant for some time. I loved it because the yard was full of flowers and big green bushes and trees. The owners must have had someone taking care of the yard while they were trying to sell it. The house used to be a bed and breakfast but now...

Once again he opened my door for me and led me up the walkway to the door. I was getting antsy, excited and a little frightened by what he might have to say. He stopped in the doorway, his hand jammed in the doorframe.

"Clara, I told you not to be scared," he said hoarsely as his mouth opened and he licked his bottom lip.

I looked at him questioningly.

"How do you know I'm scared."

"I just do. Please don't." He took a cautious step towards me. "All this is going to be hard enough and I won't be able to handle it if you're going to be frightened of me."

"You're not really helping by saying things like that."

"I know, just please try to keep calm."

"Ok," I promised. "I'll try."

I saw a cage in the corner with a huge blue and green McCaw inside. Other than the bird, there was no decorations, just old fashioned furniture that probably came with the place. The bird seemed content to gnaw on its nut so I just focused back on Eli.

"Sit," he ordered softly, but made no further movements to come near me. I sat on the sofa he directed me to and watched the emotions play over his face as he stood in the doorway. "Please promise me you won't just run. Promise that you'll hear me out first and then if you want to leave, I'll let you."

I nodded and said, "Yes. I promise." I tried to be as calm as I could muster and he took a deep breath before speaking.

"Now, I lied to you when we met about my parents living with me. They are alive but I won't live with them, though I see them from time to time even if I don't want to. My parents and my brother and sister live a different life than mine. They're cruel and sadistic. I couldn't live like that, so I ran away." He looked down at the floor and then back to me without lifting his head. "I ran away...one hundred and twenty three years ago."

I gulped and clasped my hands in my lap. Oh boy... He continued.

"I know you can believe in the supernatural. We share Reveries. I know you know that's real. Well there's lots of things in this world that you never knew existed. Supernatural things, and I'm one of them. My kind are called Devourers. My family are as well but they choose to live true to their nature and I fight mine," he spat and I could tell he truly believed what he was saying, crazy as it was. "See...we scare people, in Reveries mostly, and feed off their emotions. I don't sleep, none of us do, but I can feel every dark emotion that runs through any person I am in proximity to. Hate, jealousy, greed, pain, anger... lust. I have lived and fed on these emotions my entire life. But then you..." He shook his head and took a step forward but thought better of it. "I could feel your sorrow from across the park that day. It was unlike anything I'd ever felt before because not only could I feel your pain at your loss but when I got closer to you, I could feel your calm and contentment too; the way you were just lying there looking at the clouds made you happy. I have never in my entire existence felt those emotions before. I had no idea what was happening but then you glanced at me and looked me over...I could feel your attraction." I felt my eyes go wide and my cheeks heat but he continued. "Clara, I had to know you. I only planned to stay here a few weeks, like I usually do when I pass through a town. But you...I had to know this girl who was still happy and sweet even though she had apparently suffered so much."

I bit my lip as I looked at him. He was coiled, ready for me to take flight and bolt. His eyes begged me so I pulled it together and decided to ask questions so I could seem like I was believing until I could get out of there.

"So, you scared me that night? To feed yourself?"

"I only did it that once. I needed to see if I affected you or not but I promise you I'll never do that again. I only feed on the emotions that people feel without my interference. I don't elicit those feelings in them like my family does. Not anymore," he said sadly.

"So you can make people feel fright?"

"Yes, I can, but I don't," he insisted quickly. "Our kind can make you feel fright, hurt, sorrow, lust...but the most potent emotion is terror. It fills us up like nothing else, until I met you. Your...when you..." He actually chuckled like he was embarrassed and it was cute even though he was clearly insane. Maybe I could get him some help. "Your attraction to me, it feeds me like nothing else in this world ever has. There were rumors about your mate being able to feed you on their emotions alone but I never believed it. Until now."

"Mate?" I said, blushing furiously.

"I know, it's a dumb word," he said, rubbing the back of his neck. "I'm sorry, uh...a person who pulls you, draws you to them. I know you feel it too. I feel it every time you think about me," he said hoarsely and my pulse jumped.

That look was back; the ecstasy look. I turned the promise ring on my finger and thought about what I could do. I was pulled to him, I had wondered about that from day one; why I felt so comfortable and strange around him. But that didn't mean he was a supernatural being.

"Eli," I said cautiously. "I'm..." I had no idea what to say.

"Let me prove it to you," he said but didn't look to happy about it.

Six

"Eli-"

"How do you explain the Reveries, Clara?"

"I can't." And I couldn't. That part was definitely a mystery. "I can't, but I'm sure there's something to explain it."

"There is something to explain it. I am what I say I am."

"Eli..."

"I don't want to do this, Clara, but you have to believe me," he said and came a step closer. He knelt down in front of me. "Look at me."

"Eli-"

"Look at me," he repeated more forcefully.

I looked up into his violet eyes now level with mine and felt a little spike in my heartbeat. I squinted looking at him. Then I felt my hands begin to shake and my heart rate picked up increasingly. I suddenly felt scared for no apparent reason at all. He opened his mouth and licked his bottom lip. I chalked it all up to him freaking me out with his talk.

"I'm scared because you're freaking me out."

"No, you're scared because I made you that way."

"That's what I just said."

"No," he refuted and shook his head.

Then I felt terrified, my blood was hot out of nowhere. My heart beat painfully and my lip trembled. I looked around me, not able to just sit and not understand what was happening. Then it just stopped, like the flipping of a light switch.

My heart didn't even have to cascade to a slow, it just abruptly returned to normal beat. I jumped up, pushing him away and fell backwards until I felt the wall against my back. I slid down to the floor, my knees to my chest.

"What did you do?"

He got up and walked slowly to me, eyeing me like I was hurt animal. He pulled me to him cautiously and hugged me, his arms around me protectively as he knelt with me.

"I'm sorry. I didn't want to do that, but I had to make you see it was for real."

I felt terrified for real this time. I heard his swift intake of breath and knew he registered it. I believed him. He got what he wanted; I was frightened, but also drawn to him. What else could he do to me?

"Don't, Clara, please," he begged roughly. "I don't want to feed off you like this."

"Then don't."

"I don't have a choice!" He pulled back to look at me. "What you feel, I absorb. I can't stop it, especially the bad stuff. It soaks into my skin, my tongue, and I hate it. I don't want to feel that from you. I only want you to feel safe and happy and loved. Please, Clara, just breathe." He tucked my hair behind my ear. "Keep calm. I'm not ever going to hurt you. Understand?"

I pulled away and shifted down the wall a little to get away. I just needed to be away from him for a minute.

"Eli, I... What am I supposed to say to this?"

He looked so defeated, slumped on his knees with his hands in his lap.

"I don't know, Clara. I've never told anyone what I am before."

"Why not?"

"This is a pretty good example of why, I think," he said softly. "You're afraid of me, and I never wanted that."

"Then why'd you tell me? Why not just let me think you were a normal guy?"

"Because you deserved to know the truth, and I didn't want to spend any of my time with you living a lie. I wanted, for the first time, to be myself with someone."

I had a thought. Something he said made me think.

"You've never been with anyone else?" I asked and was surprised at how tiny my voice sounded as I pushed my legs under me, making myself small.

"No," he answered and looked over at me, his purple eyes serious. "I can't feel, Clara. I've never felt anything for anyone...until I met you."

"What do you feel with me?"

"Everything. Happiness, eagerness, friendship, sweetness, caring...love. I've never felt those things before. It's... amazing," he said in awe and smiled a small, pained smile.

I felt a breath shudder through me. I'd never told anyone I loved them before except my parents. I'd never loved anyone before. Was he saying he loved me? I barely knew him and yet, I did feel something for him. I cared about him. So I told him.

"I care about you, Eli, I do. I can feel something...between us. But what you're telling me is just crazy. I mean you...you terrify people so you can survive."

"*Terrified*. Past tense."

"You live off negative emotion…without me. That's what you're telling me?" He nodded. "I don't know, Eli. I don't know if I can handle this," I said, feeling the strain in my words as I ran my hands through my hair.

"I don't hurt people anymore. I can't help what I am, Clara. I would if I could. If I could be human I'd do anything for it, but I can't."

"I know you can't help it, but it's just...it's a lot to process."

"I'll give you all the time you need."

"And what if I can't do this?" I asked in a whisper.

He sighed and balled his fists on his knees. "Then I'll let you go and won't bother you again."

"You would?"

"Of course. I'd do anything you asked of me, Clara. Even go away."

I thought about this and knew he was sincere. I needed time to think. I didn't want him to go away but could I deal with what he was? His being next to me and my want to comfort him and wipe that rejected look off his face was confusing me. But first...

I scooted down the wall towards him. When I stopped in front of him again, he looked up at me, hopeful and eagerly watching me. I touched his face, my palm to his cheek. He felt so normal and human and real as he closed his eyes, leaning into my touch. I then let my fingers travel to his lips, his neck, then through his hair.

He huffed a breath, opening his eyes, and looked torn between agony and having everything he ever wanted. I couldn't help myself. I leaned in and kissed him. He let me though he didn't touch me back and I was grateful. I didn't know if I could leave if he did and I was about to get up and ask him to give me some thinking space.

He kept his hands on his legs, but his lips were doing plenty all their own. I kissed him once more gently, and looked up at him.

"I need some time to think. Please."

He nodded and I heard him gulp painfully.

"Anything you want. I'll stay away."

"Eli...I'm not saying this is forever. Don't leave. I just need to-"

"I'm not going anywhere," he assured me firmly. "I'll wait for you as long as I have to."

I hugged him and his arms around me were almost too much. I pulled away and walked swiftly out the door and didn't look back.

~ ~ ~

That night, I lay in bed and dreaded closing my eyes for more than one reason. One, I didn't want to see Eli and was afraid he'd be there waiting. Two, I did want to see Eli and was afraid he wouldn't come.

My white ceiling with little plaster stars above my bed was the only thing to focus on in the dark. I felt like a failure. How could I just walk out on him like that after he told me everything? He was so devastated by my reaction. But it was crazy right? A Devourer? It just sounded evil. It was evil, but he was fighting it, he told me. He didn't want to be that way. Could he really help what he was born to be? Could I blame a snake for being a snake when I really wanted a rabbit? No. And I couldn't blame Eli either…but would I play with a snake even if it wasn't his fault for being one?

Sleep found me soon enough and to my relief and dismay, Eli respected my wishes and it was the second night in weeks that I didn't see him behind my eyelids.

~ ~ ~

I thought when I woke that morning, I'd feel better or more confident about a decision. I wasn't even close. I trudged to homeroom just as the bell rang, on purpose. I didn't want to see anybody or risk the chance of running into Eli that morning. Then I scooted off to first period and skipped my locker on the way to second. Tate was waiting there for me and I so was not ready to have that conversation.

Then lunch came. Crap. As I debated going to the library instead of going in, I felt a hand on my wrist. Unexpectedly, I turned excited thinking it was Eli, but it was Tate and my heart plummeted. At least I knew how I really felt about

Eli. I still wanted him. It made me smile but Tate mistook my smile for himself and smiled back, encouraged.

"I missed you. Can we talk, babe? Please."

"I have nothing to say."

He seemed confused but pressed on.

"Clara, listen." He looked around and saw a little corner off to the side where we'd be half hidden. He took me there and pressed me in it so he had to be my warden. "I know I screwed up-" he blanched and grimaced, "sorry, bad wording, but I'm serious. I know it was dumb, but I wanted you so much and you kept refusing me and it was so frustrating. One night after I came home from your house, Dee was waiting for me. She told me she'd been in love with me forever and you stole me or something. I knew it was bull crap, but she was wearing this little red dress that-"

"Tate!" I protested. "Really? We're gonna talk about this?"

"No, listen. I was so frustrated and she seduced me. And I let her," he said ashamed. "I'm sorry. It was only supposed to be that one time but she kept sending me texts and meeting me in places unexpectedly. It just became easy to use her and get some release that way. It meant nothing." I scoffed, disgusted, but he grabbed my upper arms to keep me there. "I'm sorry. I know it was unforgiveable. I promise you it's over; never again. I'm not even going to sit with her at lunch anymore. I need you, baby. Please," he begged and tried to touch my face but I jerked away.

"I love how guys say 'it meant nothing' like that's supposed to make it all ok. You only stopped because you got caught. And Dee of all people? I can't do this Tate." I tried to leave but he stopped me by grabbing my arm. "Let go."

"Not until we talk this out."

"There's nothing left to talk about. You blew it. I can't just forget."

"Is this about Eli?" he asked angrily, his grip getting tighter and he must have seen the look on my face. "I'll murder him."

"No, this is about you, Tate. You're the one doing drugs and you're the one who cheated on me, not Eli."

He pushed me to the wall with force, not enough to hurt me but enough to scare me. And I was scared. His eyes were wild and blazing.

"Don't you ever say his name to me," he growled.

"Tate, you're hurting me."

He got right in my face, his breath on my cheek as he growled his words low.

"Well then, join the club. You don't think you're hurting me with this act? I saw you with your lips all over him this morning."

"Tate, stop." His fingers dug into my under arm.

"You think he wants you? He just wants to use you and show me that he could take you from me. The new kid trying to make a name for himself by taking down the star of the school. That's what guys like him do."

"Ow," I groaned when I could no longer hold it in. "Stop!"

"Let her go. Now," I heard behind Tate and knew it was Eli.

"I'd skip away if I were you, boy," Tate said low without looking away from me. "This is none of your business-"

"She *is* my business. Let. Her. Go."

Tate turned, keeping an arm on me, and looked at Eli over his shoulder. I finally saw him for the first time that day. He looked murderous; jaw clenched, fists balled at his sides, his hair was a mess, though cute that way, and he had his uniform button up shirt open over his white tee.

"Get lost. You can have her when I'm through with her."

Eli grabbed Tate's arm; the one holding me to the wall.

"Don't talk about her like that." He pulled Tate's arm away and I was shocked at his strength. Tate seemed to be too as he glared at Eli's hand. "Come on, Clara." He held his other hand out to me. I went gladly and got behind him. "Don't ever touch her again."

"You just made a huge mistake, foreigner."

"I don't think I did." He let go of Tate's arm and put an arm around my back to guide me. "Come on."

"Oh, nuhuh. This ain't even close to over!" Tate yelled and I heard his footsteps before seeing Tate grab Eli's shirt back.

Eli turned, with speed my eyes missed, and punched Tate's jaw, swinging him around in a 180 before he fell to the concrete floor, hard and final.

He groaned and rolled, but didn't get up.

"Come on," Eli repeated and once again put his arm behind my back as a small crowd stopped to gawk.

"Is he ok?" I asked as we walked away.

"He's fine. He'll just be embarrassed later that he was taken down by the new kid."

"Wow, Eli. They should recruit you for the wrestling team."

"Yeah," he said wryly. "I'm sure Tate would love that."

"Is that...uh, one of your supernatural things? Strength and speed?"

"Yeah," he sighed and stopped at our Math class door. "Go ahead and sit. I'll get your book."

"You don't have to- wait. You know my combination?"

"I have a keen eye and a good memory."

"So you were spying," I said and smiled to make sure he knew I was joking.

"Yeah. Sort of." He smirked and left towards my locker and I went to my seat. He came back within a minute. "Here you go."

"Aren't you scared someone will see you moving that fast?"

"I'm careful." He sat facing me in the seat across the aisle. "Are you ok? Did he hurt you?"

"No, I'm fine." I rubbed my arm thinking about it and he took it in his hand, turning it over.

His eyes went wide and his face turned red with strain. I looked down to see a few red and bruising spots where Tate had grabbed me too hard.

"I'll kill him," he muttered and went to stand. I grabbed his hand to stop him and could've sworn the veins in his arm were standing out and almost blue looking, but when I blinked again they were gone. "Clara, he can't get away with that. He hurt you. I warned you that if he hurt you again I'd-"

"Please. Please, don't. Just stay with me." I pulled him down to sit again and he looked closer at my arm.

"Are you ok? Really?"

"Yes. He just wanted to talk. Wanted me to forgive him."

"And did you?" he asked, running his finger over my bruise in angered fascination.

"Even if I did...things have changed now."

"What things?" he asked and looked at my face closely.

"Eli, you know what I'm talking about," I said softly and covered his hand with mine on his arm.

"Does that mean..." he said hopefully, gently squeezing my fingers.

"It means that I'm not going back to Tate. I'm still... working everything else out. It's crazy, Eli."

"I know," he sighed and promised, "I planned to leave you alone, I did."

"How did you know I needed you?"

"I felt someone was scared when I was walking into the cafeteria. I knew right off it was you."

That floored me. It was true, what he said last night about me being different for him. He saved me today and I didn't want to think about what Tate might have done if Eli hadn't shown up.

"Thank you for saving me," I said gently.

I pulled him to me, him seeming surprised, and just as my lips touched his cheek the door banged open and a couple rowdy students poured in, joking about Tate getting knocked out. Lunch was over. Eli leaned back and chuckled in annoyance and amusement.

"Mmmm," he groaned. "I better get in my seat. Will I see you later tonight?" he asked hopefully.

"I...I still need time to..." I said, unsure.

"No pressure."

"I'll see you in Art," I said with a smirk to lighten the mood.

He smiled and rubbed my cheek with his thumb before moving to his seat while the rest of the kids were coming in and being loud. The teacher came too, banging her pencil on the desktop to get everyone's attention. Class crept by increasingly slow, like water in a watched pot not boiling. I was anxious to get to Art to see Eli. But to my dismay, there was a note on the door telling us to go to the gym for that period because the Art teacher had an emergency. I completely forgot to do the assignment anyway.

So I went and dressed out with the girls to play volleyball. I loved volleyball and soon the class was over and I was changing and heading home.

As I walked through the door I remembered that we'd told Patrick yesterday at lunch that we might go to that club with him tonight. I wondered if Eli was going. I thought about texting Eli about it but kept going back and forth as I nibbled my carrot sticks snuck from the fridge. I did want to go but I also needed to think. I didn't want to string him along or give him the wrong idea. Though kissing his cheek today was probably doing just that. Ugh. Boys.

The babies were extremely colicky tonight. It was like God was sending me a message to get out of the house.

So, by seven o'clock, enough was enough and I decided to give the club a shot and if Eli was there, he was there. I hadn't told him I was coming so there would be no mixed signals, I hoped. And if he didn't come, then I'd try to have fun and be my own person for a change. I'd always done everything with my little band of friends. I needed to learn to do things alone and make my own friends. Besides, Patrick would be there.

So I showered quickly and put on a pair of jeans with my black heels and the dark blue and black silk peasant top that Dee claimed she saw first. It seemed to fit the night's theme of independence. With my hair left down and a little make-up, I was ready to go. I told Pastor and Mrs. Ruth where I was going. Since I was not being picked up by a boy, Pastor let me borrow his Silver Camry and send me off with his usual "be careful and be home by midnight".

I drove to the place and saw a packed parking lot so I parked on the street. I got out and started to make my way up the sidewalk but got cold feet. What was I doing there? I didn't really want to go in there by myself. I should've known I'd chicken out. Even if Patrick was inside, I didn't know him *that* well.

I turned to go back to the car and saw Eli standing by the wall near the door. I felt so relieved as I walked towards him. He looked at me but his eyes slid right past me. My steps faltered and I lost my nerve. Was he changing his mind now? He looked back to me and he stared at me for a few seconds and then he smiled. I smiled back and walked right up to him and kissed his cheek.

"Hey," I said and fingered the buttons on his shirt. It was a strange pick for him, a bright blue and white striped polo. Everything else I'd seen him in was darker and more low key. "I wondered if you were coming or not."

"Did you now?" he said smoothly in that accent of his. "And why wouldn't I come, sweetness?"

"Well...I didn't get to talk to you about coming earlier. I thought you might." I bit my lip. "Look, I know things are weird right now...but can we go inside and just have fun? I really need a night out, with no stress." I linked my arms around his middle. "Please?"

"I think I can oblige," he said and wrapped his arms around me.

"Good."

"Is this really your scene?"

"No. My crowd never hung out here. I'm trying something new. Besides, Patrick invited us, remember?"

"Hmm," he hummed and nodded. "Are you ready to go in?"

"Ready when you are."

He then bent his head to kiss me. I immediately felt warm all over and heard him groan as he turned us to press me to the wall. He kissed me for a few long seconds. "Oh, wow," he whispered against my lips. "You are exquisite."

I was just about to think about how strange he was acting when I heard my name. I peeked around Eli and saw...Eli. He seemed confused, then hurt, then angry. He glared at the man with his arms around me.

I looked up to the one with his arms still around me tightly and he grinned deviously and winked, making my fear spike as to what was going on. It was then I noticed that his eyebrow ring was missing. He opened his mouth, licked his lips and leaned forward to kiss the side of my mouth as he groaned in delight.

"Aww," fake Eli crooned. "Brother has come to spoil my fun, now hasn't he?"

Seven

"Clara," Eli said and reached his hand out to me, beckoning. "Come away from him now."

I wondered if the fake Eli would try to stop me but he lifted his hands, as if in surrender, and let me go freely. I heard him laugh as Eli pulled me behind him.

"Brother."

"Enoch," Eli spat. "What are you doing here? How did you find me?"

"You're not that hard to find anymore. You travel to these pitiful little towns and buy those quaint old houses. So pathetic and predictable."

"Eli," I asked. "What's going on?"

He sighed and took my hand behind him, almost as if to hide the fact that he was trying to comfort me.

"Clara, this is my brother, Enoch. My twin."

"One of your family that you were telling me about?"

"Yes."

"Tsk, tsk, brother," Enoch mocked. "You didn't introduce your little cupcake *to me*. How rude. Especially after I've tasted her lips and her fright, her want." He licked his lips again and smiled at me. "All were delicious."

I blushed and covered my cheek with my hand in embarrassment. I knew something had been off with Eli when I saw him there on the wall. But Eli didn't mention that his brother was a twin. How could I have known?

"Don't, Clara. You have nothing to be ashamed about," Eli whispered. He looked from me to his brother. "You thought you were kissing me, after all."

His brother laughed and pushed off from the wall.

"Ouch." Then he shook his head in mock disappointment. "I can't believe you told a human about what you are. I'm in delightful shock - both by your actions and her reaction. She still wanted to kiss you after you told her you siphon off her emotions. Fascinating." Eli just continued to glower. "Goodbye, brother. Bye, Clara. Nice, uh...meeting you. I hope we can meet again. Maybe next time, you can leave the stick in the mud at home."

Eli growled and Enoch laughed again as he disappeared around the corner of the building.

Eli's visibly relaxed and turned to me.

"Are you ok?" he asked as his hands roamed my arms and face. "He didn't hurt you did he? What happened?"

"I saw you - I thought it was you - waiting here. So I walked up to you and said I was wondering if you'd be here. Then you kissed me..." I shook my head. "I'm sorry."

"Why are you apologizing?"

"I kissed him back," I confessed.

"It was me you were kissing." He smiled and ran his thumb over my bottom lip. "I should be happy you want to kiss me at all. What happened to thinking it over? I didn't think I'd see you here tonight."

"I'm still thinking but...I can't seem to keep away from you. I was hoping you'd be here," I admitted. "Can we just take things slow? I'm still not sure what's going on...with everything, but I want to still be friends."

"That's sounds really good, actually." He glanced behind us. "Do you still want to go in or…"

"Yeah, we might as well. We're here."

Eli bent down to kiss my forehead, holding my face gently. I felt a tap on my shoulder and turned to see Patrick.

"You both made it. Awesome." He hugged me and told me I looked great in my ear. "Let's go in. You can suck face on the inside of the club too, ya know," he said grinning and bumped fists with Eli as he chuckled.

The bouncer asked for all our I.D.s and I started to wonder when he asked if they were going to let me in or not. I hadn't thought it would be a problem.

"You can't come in," he confirmed my fears. "Eighteen and up only, kid."

"You're not eighteen?" Patrick asked. "But you're a senior."

"I have an early birthday. I don't turn eighteen until May."

"Dang."

"Let her in," Eli said, looking at the bouncer closely. "Let. Her. In."

The bouncer blinked a few times and looked around. Then he looked back to me.

"Go ahead. But if someone asks, you snuck in, got it?"

"Yes. Thank you," I answered.

"Eli, dude. Awesome. You got some Jedi mind tricks working for you, man," Patrick praised as we followed him in.

I looked at Eli, but he wouldn't meet my gaze. Inside, the music was so loud it actually vibrated through me, making my vision bounce and it was impossible to hear. So much for talking anything out with Eli tonight. We went to the bar and ordered a few sodas. It didn't escape my notice how Eli's protective arm stayed around me the entire time.

The announcer said that the first band of the night, Blue Ashes, was about to take the stage. Eli pointed to the balcony, asking if I wanted to go there with him. I nodded. Patrick and his boys followed us and Eli leaned me against the railing and caged me in with his arms from behind me.

It made me smile because he was protective in a fierce way that was unlike Tate. Tate had been protective like I was a possession of his. Eli was protective like I was something precious.

I turned to look at him and found his face right there over my shoulder. My cheek touched his lips and nose. He kissed it and I shivered. I felt him exhale on my face and realized I was feeding him right that second. I tried to calm down, taking a deep breath. It was kind of chilly inside the smoky club actually, which was weird. I took Eli's arms and put them around me without even thinking.

"I promise I'm not playing some stupid girly flirting game. I'm just cold. Is this ok?" I asked loudly.

"Are you kidding me?" he said into my ear and kissed my cheek once more. "And you look stunning, by the way. I didn't really get a chance to say that before."

"Thank you. So do you."

He laughed. "Never been called stunning before."

"Well, you are."

He smiled and chuckled silently, but I could feel him shake slightly. He put his head against mine for a few seconds and then the lights went out completely. The show was starting.

The band was terrible, but in the strobing and laser lights Patrick and his friends seemed to enjoy them. Then another band came and played a small set, then another. I wasn't too impressed with any of them but it was still fun to watch and entertaining. And Eli's arms around me made it even better.

Finally ten o'clock rolled around and I really wanted to talk to Eli. I pulled him to me and yelled as much in his ear. He must have gotten the gist because after he motioned to Patrick that we were leaving. He held my hand tightly and towed me down the stairs and out the door.

"Where'd you park?" Eli asked looking around furiously, for the car or Enoch I didn't know, and I showed him.

"Where are you parked?" I asked.

"I walked. I'll just ride with you if that's ok."

"Yeah, of course. I'm sorry if you wanted to stay, I just really wanted to talk to you."

"No," he opened the passenger door to my car, put me in and then got in the driver's seat, "I wanted to leave too. I need to explain some things to you about my brother."

"Ok, good, because I have some questions."

"Where to?" he asked as he pulled a swift u-turn onto the highway.

"Not home. Let's go to the dock, out past the warehouse district."

"Alright. Buckle up."

He drove us quickly and I decided to start the questioning.

"So, I thought you said your kind couldn't feel? If that's the case, then why did Enoch kiss me?"

"Our bodies feel, just not those kinds of emotions. Not love but lust. Not friendship but competition. My brother has always been somewhat of a female conqueror," he said and I could tell he thought it was disgusting.

"So he seduces girls just to feed off them? And then leaves?"

"Pretty much. He gets what he wants and needs. He's not made to care about the person. I'm not making excuses for him," he said quickly. "I'm just saying, Devourers don't have relationships, even with each other. It's all twisted and dysfunctional. It's not real. It's all a game, a show."

"So what's he doing here?"

"Good question," he muttered as he pulled into the dirt road and I showed him where to park. "I haven't seen him in about five years."

We sat in the car and looked out at the water. The long list of things I wanted to ask were a jumbled mess in my head. I couldn't seem to make sense of any of it.

"Ok. So, what happens now? You skip town because he found you?"

He looked at me with a face of horror.

"No, Clara. No. He'll leave soon enough on his own. He bores easily. I'm not leaving you," he took my hand, "unless you send me away."

"I don't want you to go away." I gnawed my lip as he rubbed my knuckles with his thumb. "So what's up with him? Why does he follow you around?"

"I told you, it's a game. And if we see him again, which I'm hoping we won't, but if we do, I'll have to pretend like I'm just using you so he'll leave you alone."

"What?" I said not understanding.

"If he knows how I really feel about you, he'll just try to torment you and I can't have that. He'll know that something is different about you. I'll have to be with you at night, in your Reveries, so he can't get in. We'll just keep a low profile until I know he's gone."

"Low profile. Sounds very 007." He laughed and I smiled, loving hearing it. "Ok, so you ignore me and hope he leaves, that's taken care of. Now. How old are you?"

He seemed surprised by the question, and I bet he'd never been asked before where he could actually tell the truth.

"Uh...three hundred, plus some. I lost count."

I gulped and fidgeted with my ring. "You don't remember the year you were born?"

"Mother wasn't too keen on keeping records," he said and laughed without humor. "My brother, sister and I were just a means to keep our race going after all."

"That's terrible."

"Not really. We just don't view family like humans do. Trust me, if you knew my parents you'd be glad they cut me loose."

I thought about that and felt like he was being a little ungrateful. At least he still had his parents. I missed mine so much. My face must have shown my sadness, or he felt it maybe.

"Ah, I'm sorry, Clara. I didn't mean to be so callous. I just meant that they are a ruthless pair, nothing like I'm sure your parents were with you."

"It's ok." I absorbed that, trying not to shudder. "So, you came to the club. I didn't think you would."

"I didn't think you would either, but I didn't want to miss the chance that you might."

"I'm glad you did." I shook my head. "I can't believe I couldn't tell that wasn't you."

"He knew you thought he was me. That's all that mattered. If I hadn't shown up he would have just pretended until you realized it. And then..." He shook his head furiously. "No, I'm not thinking about that."

"He didn't seem...I don't know, evil. He was a jerk, but he seemed…he seemed normal, like you."

"What did he say to you?"

"I told him I didn't think you were coming. He said why wouldn't he come. I said I knew things were weird but could we just try to have fun tonight and not worry about everything. He said he would and then he kissed me. He stopped and said...I was exquisite." I cringed looking at Eli. "Wow, you're exquisite."

"He said that?" Eli asked and seemed shocked. "That was the words he used?"

"Yeah. Why?"

"Nothing. It's just strange. He doesn't usually comment, he just takes what he wants and leaves. Maybe he's just playing with me. Never mind." He waved his hand before taking mine in his. "If you see him just ignore him. He won't play if it's not fun."

"So...this is how all Devourers live? Having random kisses and just eating emotion from strangers all day and night?"

"Mostly, yes. But...I don't...anymore." He sighed and rubbed his face with his free hand. "I haven't lived like that in a very long time. I survive on strangers but they don't even know I'm doing it. I just find ones that are sad or angry. It made things a lot harder on me but...I've survived that way, albeit it uncomfortably and near severe hunger sometimes; to try to atone for what I've done."

"Eli..." My heart was breaking for him. He was so guilty, his fingers were actually shaking in my hand. "That's over." As much as I didn't want to think about the things he'd done before, especially with other girls, I knew it wasn't his fault. He was fighting it. "Eli, look at me." I pulled his face up when he didn't. "I don't blame you. You've changed, that's what matters. What happened? What made you decide to be different?"

"I don't know, really." He smiled. "I was walking into a diner one day and a little boy bumped into my leg. I was so annoyed and when I looked down to see him looking up at me, just as annoyed as I was, I laughed. For the first time in my entire existence...I laughed out of pure enjoyment. I'd never felt that emotion before. I watched him walk away with his mother and I thought about how hard it would be to hurt him after that, to make him scared and feed off him, and I knew I couldn't. From that day on, I never forced an emotion onto another person unless it was necessary. That's why I liked your Josiah so much the other day. It reminded me of that boy who saved me," he said and smiled again remembering. "But I never felt another good emotion after that day, until I met you. Now I can't stop feeling it around you. It's all over you."

"So I'm your muse," I said and smiled coyly.

"That's a very good description. My muse, Clara Belle," he breathed and ran his fingers down my cheek.

"So how do you know my middle name?"

"I saw it in your school file. That secretary's office is very nicely decorated-"

"Eli!" I laughed. "You broke into the school?"

"Technically, I was already in the school. I broke into her office." He smiled gorgeously at me. "I had to know you," he admitted and shrugged.

I leaned over and put my head on his chest. Some girls might be upset about him digging through their files. I was just glad he cared enough to go to the trouble. He sighed happily and ran his fingers through my hair. It felt so good. For the first time in days, I felt like everything was ok and maybe working out for the best.

"So, do you have more questions for me?" he spoke into my hair.

"Tons, but I can't seem to work my brain right now."

"Well, can I ask one thing?"

"Sure."

"Can I have the kiss that was supposed to be mine anyway?"

I looked up at him and smiled. He turned my face up towards him and pressed his lips to mine gently. I pulled back a little.

"I...don't want to lead you on."

"You're not. I know what I'm getting into. I can be patient, I told you."

"I've been called a tease before," I muttered thinking about Tate and then regretting it.

"You are not a tease. I asked for it didn't I? I won't get the wrong idea, I'm glad to spend any time with you I can get. Sometimes...a kiss is just that."

Devour - Shelly Crane

I pulled him back to me and let him ravish my mouth furiously, turning in my seat to reach him better. His breaths were huffing like we were running a marathon and he groaned several times as my skin heated and he absorbed the want I felt for him and my happiness at the situation for the moment. It was odd to think that I was essentially feeding him what he needed to survive. When I ran my hand through his hair his grip tightened on me and he pulled me closer and I let him kiss me deeper.

I let him devour me.

Eight

After Eli took me home, ten minutes before curfew, he walked to his house despite my protest to drive him. He assured me he'd be fine and waited for me to go inside. I was glad the Pastor and Mrs. Ruth weren't waiting for me. I'd just had one of the longest make out sessions of my life, case being, because I didn't have to stop him, and I'm sure I had that just-been-kissed look. Unlike Tate, he didn't try to push me too far, didn't try to ply me with sweet nothings as he reached for skin under my clothes.

It was heavenly to feel safe in more ways than one.

He did tell me he'd see me in the dark so I wasted no time trying to get to bed. That night, he took me back to the park. It was daytime again and we sat and counted cloud animals as we lay in the grass. I lay my head on his stomach and ran my fingers over his eyebrow piercing. Once again, he walked me home when it was over and kissed me on my porch.

The next morning, I woke feeling giddy and refreshed. I was ready to get to school. I hadn't wanted to go to school in a very long time. After putting on a sweater with my uniform skirt, I made my way down for breakfast.

"Hey, sweetie," Mrs. Ruth said as she scooped and cut pancakes onto plates. "How was your night? I was pooped so I went to bed early."

"It was good. I was home at eleven something, I promise."

"We trust you, I just wanted to see if you had fun."

"Yes, ma'am. I did have fun. Eli showed up."

"You seem to mention him a lot lately," she said with clear inflection as she passed me a big plate of flap jacks with extra butter, just the way I liked them.

"Yes, ma'am," I agreed and left it at that. "Thanks for breakfast."

"Of course. The munchkins have to eat anyway. Hannah, wipe your mouth." When Hannah gave her a sulky look, Mrs. Ruth gave her a do-it-now look herself. Hannah wiped her mouth, with the quickness. "So, how are the new classes? Do you have any with Tate?"

"Just homeroom. I like them all fine."

"And how are things with him?" she asked and I heard her disapproving tone.

"I'm not seeing him anymore. He cornered me one day and…well, Eli came to my rescue."

"What?" She dropped the fork she was using and fumbled to recover it. "What happened?"

"Nothing. It's ok. It wasn't a big deal."

She thought for a second, chewing her pinky nail.

"Do you want Pastor to talk to the principal about switching homerooms?"

"No, it's ok. I'm not going to run from him."

"But it would be better, I think. I heard some rumors, Clara, going around town. Steroids? Please tell me it's not true."

I put my fork down mid-bite and sighed.

"It's true." She gasped and covered her heart so I went on. "He claimed he was only doing it for the meets, the championships. His dad puts a lot of stress on him. I told him no more but the last time I saw him he…well, let's just say he wasn't very nice. I accused him of still taking them and he didn't deny it. So, I told him it was over but he didn't take the news too well."

"Clara! You should have called us! I'm surprised the school didn't."

"They didn't know. Eli…he punched Tate," I admitted and scrunched my nose at her look. "It was in my defense."

"Clara, this is serious. This should have been reported!"

"Eli just ushered me to class and made sure I was ok. I didn't even think about it. It's fine. I think Tate's pride was hurt enough for him to forget about me."

"This is all very scandalous," she sighed and shook her head. "I have to tell Pastor but I'll keep it low key." She gave me a look with twisted lips. "He's not going to be happy about this, especially after what happened at the match."

"I know. I didn't want to worry you guys."

"It's not your fault but it needs to be addressed."

"If you say so," I said softly. "I'd rather just forget it myself."

"How easy is it going to be to forget when homeroom starts in," she looked at the clock, "seventeen minutes?"

"Crap, I gotta go," I said quickly and chugged my milk. "See you guys."

"Clara, please be careful. I worry about you."

"I'm fine," I assured her. "Bye, munchkins."

"Bye, Clara!" a sweet chorus sang behind me as I made a mad dash to grab my cell and blot on some lip gloss.

I tossled my locks and ran to the door, only to be caught by Pastor.

"Hey, running late?"

"A little."

"Wouldn't be running off to see a certain dashing young man, now would you?"

"Maybe," I said coyly, causing him to laugh, and kissed his cheek. "Bye!"

"Have a good day, sweetheart."

"I'm sure I will!" I called and barely looked both ways before running across the street.

I thought how strange things were. I was never really close to our pastor and his wife before this. I went to church along with my parents but I never really participated. It was just something I'd always done. Now, however, they really were like parents to me. Pastor worked a lot. A lot. But what did you expect from a Pastor? That was how it should be. And they practiced what they preached. They were the sweetest, nicest, most sincere people I'd ever known in my life. I was extremely blessed that they offered to take me in instead of putting me in foster care. I would always be grateful to them for that. And though I missed my parents with an ache that still stung and burned in my chest and made my eyes prick, I was as happy as I could be in my situation. And I knew that when I peeked back at the house, Pastor would still be there watching to make sure I made it safely. I turned and there he was. I waved and smiled. He waved too and took that as his cue to go back to his work.

I waved to a few people I knew and hastily made my way inside. I had to get to my locker before homeroom. I almost growled when one of the girls from the Spirit Squad stopped me.

"Clara, hey. How. Are. You?" she said in her biggest sympathy voice. It rankled me because that was exactly how people talked to me after my parents died.

"Fine. Why wouldn't I be?"

"Well, I heard about everything that's been going on with Tate. And now Eli. Boy, you sure are busy, huh?"

"What does that mean?" I asked as the hair on my neck rose and buzzed with annoyance.

"Nothing," she said innocently and flipped her long chestnut hair, "but you can't really blame Tate for hitting Eli, can you? After he found you out like that?"

"Found out what?" I said suddenly very intrigued.

"That you were seeing Eli behind his back. I heard all about it; how he punched Eli by the cafeteria."

I sighed and felt my lips pull back in a sneer.

"Get your facts straight, Brittany. I wasn't seeing Eli behind Tate's back, for one. For another, Eli hit Tate, not the other way around."

"Oh, well, Dee is telling everyone that you were caught at the away showers with Eli and that Tate went ballistic."

I felt my jaw drop and all I could do was stare. Dee was a real piece of work. How dare she? Who did she think she was? I realized Brittany was still going and I'd missed half of the conversation.

"And so anyway, I was like, Mike, please. There's no way Eli's head went all the way around."

"Ok," I stopped her. "Now Mike?"

"Yeah. They told the whole cafeteria what happened. Poor Eli. I hope his nose grows back straight."

I almost laughed.

"Stop listening to them, Brittany. Just because the words are uttered from their lips doesn't mean it's golden."

"So, it's true? They kicked you out of their group?"

"I left," I confirmed.

"And Eli and Dee aren't dating anymore?"

"They never were!" I yelled and then bit my lip.

"Sorry," she groaned. "Look, you are apparently strung out about this whole thing, so I'll see you later."

"I'm not strung out, I'm just sick of it all."

"They're your friends," she reasoned.

"No, they never were. They were just the people I was stuck with." I looked at her closely. She was a Sophomore. I felt it was my duty to enlighten her. "Brittany, listen. This is going to sound very after-school special but just listen. High school doesn't matter. I thought it did. I thought being popular was important. I thought having a hot guy be your boyfriend and everybody knowing your name was awesome but it isn't. It gets old and it gets pointless. Don't follow them just because you think you have to. Be your own person." She gave me the weirdest look, like I was shooting green slime from my ears. I sighed. "Ok, thanks for telling me but everything they said was a total lie. Dee's just jealous and Tate's pride is hurt. See you at the pep rally later?"

Her eyes lit up again and she smiled.

"Totally! And don't worry about Tate. Eli is so much hotter anyway. Tootles!"

There was no way to reach her. My old friends were like a tractor beam; a total façade of coolness and success. I couldn't really blame her. I used to be exactly like her.

I rubbed my eyes as I pushed through the people to get to my locker. Eli was there waiting for me. I sighed in relief and it made me smile that it was an instantaneous reaction. I really did like him and wanted to be with him.

"Hey, gorgeous," he said languidly and scooted over so I could open my locker door.

"Hey," I said and looked up at him. "Have you heard the news?"

"About Tate dismantling my face? Yep." He rubbed a hand down his cheek. "Feels smooth enough to me."

I laughed.

"Yeah. Smooth." I grabbed my notebook, took a quick look into my magnetic mirror and shut it easily. "So, how was the rest of your night?"

"Good enough, I guess," he said and let his arm surround me. He whispered in my ear. "Could've been better."

I pulled back and smiled at him but it faded away. I don't know how I knew, he looked exactly like Eli. Exactly. He'd even gotten his eyebrow pierced, which was freaky enough in its own right. He saw the change come over me and smirked.

"Dang. What gave me away? Was it my suggestive tone or debonair looks?"

"How did you get in here?" I asked and tried to pull away but he held tight.

He gave me a sardonic look. Oh yeah, public school with an emphasis on the 'public'. Our small town wasn't bad boned enough for metal detectors or security guards.

"Ok, fine. How did you get a uniform? And what's up with the eyebrow? It's creepy."

"You don't look happy to see me, Clara," he sang and when I tried to pull away this time, he let me go. "I don't want any trouble."

"Really? Then what are you doing here? And how did you know all about that Tate stuff?"

"Well, I've been here all morning waiting for you to come. Everyone apparently knows Eli and have been giving me their condolences all morning. Don't worry," he assured, "I kept his precious reputation in tact and acted appropriately shocked at the revelation that a human boy could lay me out flat."

"That's not what happened," I told him, my voice raising in annoyance at the thought that everyone was talking about Eli. I kind of wanted to smile. I'd never been the protective type before. "Eli is the one who… You know, what? Never mind. You still didn't answer my question." I crossed my arms over my chest to seem more confident when really I was shaking because I realized I was now in an empty hallway with a Devourer who hadn't suddenly grown a conscious like another one I knew. The bell must have been about to ring. "What are you doing here?"

"Eli. He needs to come back and stop this ruse. It's been years. Many. Way too long to play the sullen runaway child."

"Maybe he doesn't want to go back," I countered. "Maybe he likes it here."

"With a snack like you hanging on his sleeve, I'm sure he does," he replied wryly, his accent still perplexing me to place it. "That's beside the point."

"Why? Why can't he just be rogue?"

He chuckled. "I can't believe he told you everything. It's so out of character for him." He moved forward to stand over me, his chest almost bumping mine and my pulse jumped. He licked his bottom lip and smiled. "But as I said before, you are unlike anything I've ever tasted. Maybe that's why he stays." He twitched his head to the side. "Doesn't want to lose his little candy store...do you, brother?"

I peeked over his shoulder to see Eli staring daggers into Enoch's back. I blinked to clear my vision because it seemed like Eli's veins were standing out...and blue almost. When Enoch looked back too, Eli's face changed to one of boredom.

"Enoch, leave her alone." He came forward and pulled me to him. He kissed the corner of my mouth then dragged his lips to the place under my jaw. My breath caught as my heart spiked and they both sighed. Eli then let his tongue touch my skin and he groaned before pushing me a little with his arm. "Go to class, Clara. I'll see you at lunch." The bell rang. He smacked me on the side of my thigh right as I was about to turn.

Oh no he-

His eyes pleaded. He begged me with them to just do what he said. Oh yeah. The whole Enoch-can't-know-how-I-feel-about-you thing. I sucked it up and made my way to class. I even turned at my homeroom door and winked at Eli. Even though I kind of wanted to slap him a little, I also understood. But I so didn't want to leave him like that. I felt like there was a good chance I'd never see him again. He nodded his head to my class for me to go. I went, begrudged. And I was late.

I felt Tate's gaze on me but I refused to look his way as the teacher eyed me with pursed lips. Homeroom only had a few minutes left. I was really anxious to see Eli and find out what happened. The school's morning news was blaring a story about the drinks getting spiked at the last formal and at the upcoming Homecoming Dance, this would not be tolerated. Yeah right.

The bell rang and I dashed to the hall to find it devoid of Eli. Or Enoch. Dang.

Nine

I jumped and squealed when someone put their arm around my shoulder. It was Eli…I thought.

"It's me," he assured and smiled. That genuine smile alone let me know who it was.

"What happened?" I asked and put my arms around his neck. "I was worried."

"Clara, he can't hurt me."

"Then why are you so afraid of him?"

"I'm not afraid of him, I'm afraid of what he'll do. I don't want you to be in danger because he wants to play with me."

"Would he really hurt me?" I asked and leaned back to see his face.

"I don't want to think about that answer," he said softly. "Let's go to class."

He visibly shook himself as if to be rid of the images or thoughts we had conjured. Then he once again put his arm around my shoulders and we made our way through the throngs of students. I saw Sarah, who studiously avoided me, even after I waved at her.

~ ~ ~

We walked to lunch together and once again I dreaded it, but Eli was oblivious and gently led me to the line and paid for my food, once again. We made our way out to the table and Patrick waved us over. I gave in, feeling the heat of hateful gazes on me, and saw Tate there at my old table. Dee wasn't all over him though. She was all over Mike. Gross. She was kissing Mike, eyes wide open, and staring at Tate, begging him to look and be jealous. Sad poor girl. It must be miserable to live that way.

Eli called me back to reality with a hand on my lower back. He leaned to whisper in my ear.

"Don't spend another minute of your life worrying over them," he commanded softy and kissed my cheek.

"Gross, you two," Patrick chimed. "I'll have to kiss Ike to keep up with you if you don't tone it down."

"Dude. No," Ike said in horror, as if that scenario would ever actually play out.

Everyone laughed and I took a bite of my mac-n-cheese, leaning into Eli's side. I laughed as he plowed through his bowl. For a guy that wasn't human, he could sure put away the food. That thought stopped me in my tracks.

He wasn't human.

What kind of future could I have with a guy like that? Would we get married one day? Could he have kids? Would they be what he is if we did? Could I be with him knowing I'd get old and die and he'd just watch me do it?

Eli's arm jerked on my back and he sucked in a long breath.

"Stop, Clara. Please," he begged in a whisper into my neck. "Why are you all of a sudden so upset?"

"Nothing," I answered.

"Clara-"

"Not here."

He nodded and leaned back in his chair. He took a few deep breaths and then smiled uneasily at something someone at the table was saying. I turned back to my plate and tried to relax. I didn't understand why I was only now thinking of those things. But I was young, why was I worried about them? I didn't really believe in forever anymore anyway. Things and people can be taken from you whether you wanted them to be or not. I was tired of being attached to things and them leaving or turning out to not be what I thought.

~ ~ ~

The rest of the day was a blur. I tried to not think and just focus on my teachers and schoolwork but it was kind of impossible with Eli in every class. In Art we had to draw a pencil sketch of one of our football teams helmets. You'd think that would be easy but it wasn't. At least not for me. I peeked at Eli's as he was done…and it was a masterpiece. If a perfect portrait of a football helmet could be called that.

"What's with you today?" he asked as he caught me looking.

"Nothing. What?" I said nonchalantly as I began to draw again.

I was struggling to put it mildly. Without a word he put his hand over mine on the pencil. He showed me how to turn it lower and sideways to make my short strokes. It smoothed out the lines instead of it being so fine and choppy.

"Thanks," I told him. His arm went to the back of my chair, his heat was almost a tangible thing. "I suck at this."

"No, you don't."

"Major suckage," I disagreed.

He laughed and again guided my hand easily, not cheating and doing it for me, but showing me how to do it myself. He had a way of doing things so sweetly and carefully. It was intriguing.

"Mr. Thames," the teacher called, "are you finished?"

"Yes, ma'am, I am," he sang.

"Well, thank you for helping the less fortunate students."

"Hey," I muttered, vexed, but Eli just nodded to her and chuckled in my ear.

"You are not less fortunate. She just envies the talent in her classroom all day. She's jealous of youthful, steady fingers."

"Well, she's not jealous of me," I assured and looked at the picture. "Though with your help, Picasso, that may change. Thank you."

"You are absolutely welcome," he said and then inched a little closer. "Do you want to come over tonight?"

"Nuhuh."

"Nuhuh?" he repeated disbelievingly. "What does that mean?"

"It means no," I said with a giggle.

"I know what it means, you tart, I meant what do you mean?"

"I mean that tonight is reruns of Buffy....or Vampire Diaries...or Angel. Take your pick."

"I'm assuming these are television shows that portray the teenage angst and drama of high school whilst throwing in supernatural twists and danger?"

"Exactly," I said amused.

"And you're going to watch them tonight instead of coming to hang out with me?" he said incredulously. "Alone?"

"Eli, you're cute, but you are no Salvatore."

"I'm going to guess that you just insulted me," he muttered dryly.

I burst out laughing and the teacher asked if she needed to move me. I shook my head and ducked behind his arm to stop the giggle. I thought for a second if what I was about to say would be ok. I had only ever brought home Tate as a dating material kind of boy before to the Pastor's house.

"Why don't you come over and watch it with me?" I suggested.

"You are serious aren't you? What is so great about it?"

"Come over tonight and I'll show you," I countered.

He thought, his lips curling and twisting. I saw when I'd won. I could practically read on his face that he thought I was going to be trouble for him pertaining to getting my way. I smiled and kind of liked that idea. What girl wouldn't?

"Alright, Clara Belle, you win. Can I at least take you to dinner?"

"Why don't you just eat with us tonight? Mrs. Ruth won't mind and she cooks enough food to feed a small army. She loves guests and this way they can get to know you a little and be really comfortable with my being with you all the time. Please?" I begged and smiled.

He seemed perturbed. I gave him a questioning look.

"I'm just thinking that it's going to be impossible to say no to you. I've never in my life not been in control before," he mused looking around the room. "It's very strange."

"I'm sorry?" I asked, not sure of his meaning.

He looked back at me and his smile broke all forms of concentration for me.

"I just meant that I've never wanted to give anyone anything. I've never done something for anyone or wanted to constantly be with someone. I've never been human before."

"Well, I like you like this."

"You only like me because you're getting your way," he said grinning.

"That is absolutely not true," I taunted. "Although, I'm going to talk you into many things in the days to come," he chuckled but I kept going, "I also enjoy your company."

I smiled angelically and batted my eyelashes over exaggeratedly. He smiled, too, and softly played with my fingers under the table on my leg.

"I'm very much looking forward to it," he said in a deep rumble.

I felt my cheeks tinge with pink a little and turned the promise ring on my finger so I'd have something to do. He smirked and looked up when the bell rang.

"Ok, I'll meet you there in a little while. I have to go home and feed the bird," he said.

"I forgot to ask you about that," I mused. "You have a bird. That just seems strange for you."

"It's not actually my bird. It's a long story. Cavuto is a nasty little piece of work that I would gladly be rid of."

"Ok," I dragged out, not completely understanding. "Cavuto is the bird's name? Who names a bird that?"

"Come on, Clara," he edged the topic away and pulled me from my chair. "The faster we go, the faster I can meet you at your house."

"Ok," I agreed reluctantly and grabbed my bag from the floor. "I'll prep the fam for your arrival," I said playfully.

"Sweet."

He kissed my cheek and lingered for a moment. I felt my pulse speed but before I could hear the tell tale intake of his breath at my reaction, the teacher cleared her throat and hastily ejected us from the classroom.

He walked me to the street and then left for his house. I was just about to cross the four lane when someone said my name to get my attention behind me. I turned to see two girls, or Goddesses I should say. One was an Artemis of a girl with blazing red hair and big gold earrings. Her long white dress, belted with a gold and brown belt, reached her ankles. The other girl had long blond hair down to the small of her back and her tiny tank top showed her mid drift.

Her smile was a cruel copy of Dee's and I felt my guard immediately snap to attention.

"Yes?"

"You're Clara, right?"

"Yes," I said cautiously and folded my arms. "Who are you?"

The Artemis smiled and stepped forward a bit. She held her hand out to me.

"I'm Angelina. You go to school here?"

I looked at the books in my arm and back to her, trying to not show on my face how stupid that question had been.

"Yep."

"Then I think…you've met my fiancé, Eli."

Ten

My heart stopped. My hand dropped before it even reached her.

"Eli," I repeated. "You're engaged to Eli?"

"More than engaged really," the other girl said. "They've known each other since they were kids. They were practically betrothed at birth. Isn't that sweet?" she crooned and extended her hand. I took hers this time. "I'm Mara. He doesn't know we're in town. It's a surprise."

"It will be a surprise, I think," I mused and tried to smile when all I wanted to do was hurl. "You know where he lives?"

"Yeah, we're just headed to his place now." She nudged the other girl and started to push her the way of Eli's house. "Nice to meet you, Clara. Maybe we'll see you around? We'll be in town for a few days."

"Yeah," my mouth said but my head said heck no. I swallowed hard and took a deep breath. "Bye."

Eli was engaged, to a freaking gorgeous creature who was surprising him at his house as we speak. And he didn't tell me. I marched across the street and slammed the door too hard. Harder than I wanted to but everyone was too busy to care.

My room was not the emotionless haven I wanted but I took it. I plopped face down on the bed and buried my face in my pillow. I wanted to cry but I refused. If I started, I'd spend all night doing so. It felt silly to cry over a guy I'd only known for a couple weeks anyway. But I just felt so connected to him. He cared about me, protected me, thought about me, he visited me at night when I closed my eyes and took me to sweet places. What other guy had ever done any of that and didn't want anything in return?

The doorbell interrupted my internal tirade. I got up and glanced in the mirror. Ugh. I'd cried anyway. I wiped the smeared mascara from under my eyes and smoothed my hair back. The doorbell sounded again and I rolled my eyes and bolted down the hall, grumbling out loud.

"I'm sorry. I forgot I'm the only one in this house equipped to answer the door." Just then I saw Mrs. Ruth with peas smeared down her shirt, one kid on her hip and another one crying at her feet for more Goldfish crackers. "Sorry," I told her, because she had definitely heard me mumbling. "I'll get it."

"Thank you."

She made her way back to the kitchen and I opened the door and ...what the...the nerve!

"Eli? What are you doing here?" I asked harshly and almost slammed the door in his face when I saw him register how upset I was. His mouth opened, his eyes blinked, staying shut a little too long to be normal. "Stop it!" I snapped.

"You're doing it, not me," he countered. "What is wrong with you? I told you I'd come over after I took care of some things at the house. Did I take too long or something?" Then he inched forward a little and his voice dropped to sympathetic levels. "Are you crying? What happened?"

He looked genuinely clueless. It had to be an act. He was apparently an Oscar award winner because he'd fooled me this whole time.

"Are you through with your visitor so soon?"

"What? What visitor?"

"You can drop it now, Eli. She told me."

"Who?" he asked, but then his face turned hard and I knew he knew. "Who?" he asked again, but harder and even held the door open further with a hand.

"Who do you think?" I asked softly, begging myself to not cry in front of him. "Your fiancé."

His face took a shocked direction and that was confession enough for me. I slammed the door and ran back down the hall. He didn't ring the door bell again like I thought he might. Well, that was it. He knew I knew and he was done with me. Good riddance. Boys!

That was what my head said, but the rest of me was devastated.

Was I not worth it? Was I not something that a guy would find precious and worth the trouble of being honest and straight forward with? Mike had always been a jerk to me and every other female on the planet. Tate had been good to me, but only to my face. Behind my back he was a cheating abusing idiot. And Eli. I thought I'd finally found someone who was going to be completely mine. I knew his secret! I thought that meant I was in a class all by myself, but apparently not.

I twisted the promise ring on my finger; the promise ring my mother had given me and made me promise her I'd follow it. She told me her and Dad's story. About how she wished that they had waited until they'd gotten married but luckily, they'd still only ever been with each other. She said how it felt like her wedding night had been robbed from her because it was just like every other night, nothing special. She bought me this ring and made me promise.

I wondered if I'd ever find a guy who respected and loved me enough to want to wait for me. Instead, I found boys who lied and cheated and snuck around. It was ridiculous how much they didn't care about my feelings at all. I felt so alone. I wanted to break down my mom's bedroom door and fall into her lap to cry. Or knock on Dad's office and sit on his couch with him while he scratched my head and listened to me babble. But that was no longer an option for me and it sucked royally.

I decided to call my sister. We were never really close, but I needed to talk to someone, anyone. And these days, it seemed to be slim pickings.

"Fannie?" I said when she answered.

"Don't call me that," she grumbled. "You know I hate it when you call me that."

"Sorry, Fay. Old habits."

"What's up?" she asked and I could tell she didn't really want to be talking to me.

"I, uh…I just wanted to talk."

"About what? I'm a little busy."

"About…do you miss Mom and Dad?"

"What kind of question is that? Of course I do."

"Do you miss me?" I asked. Her silence was a ringing in my ears. "I miss you. I know we weren't really close, but I miss having you around."

"Pastor's treating you good, right?"

"Of course."

"Then you've got nothing to complain about. You got lucky. Some of us had to fend for ourselves," she said bitterly.

And there it was. The reason she had barely spoken two words to me since our parents death. She was angry that I got a place to stay and she had to re-enlist in the military, because she had no where else to go.

"I'm very grateful to them but I'm also a minor. I'm still in school. I'm not being treated better than you, I wasn't given special privileges. Stop playing martyr, Fay. You always tried to act like I was spoiled."

"You were spoiled, but that's beside the point. I'm busy, I'm gonna go."

"Whatever," I grumbled.

"Look," she sighed in exasperation, "I'm working, ok? I'll call you later if you really need to talk to me and aren't just sulking about a boy or something."

"That's what sisters are supposed to be for," I countered.

"Not me. Bye, Clara."

"Bye," I said but she'd already hung up.

So, I hurriedly tried Addison's number. If I didn't get someone to talk to, I didn't know what I'd do. Although, Addison hadn't talked to me a whole lot since my parents died. She thought I blamed her on some subconscious level and avoided me like the uncomfortable situation I was. But I still felt like I could call her. So I tried.

It rang and rang. Then she picked up.

"Clara? Something wrong?"

"No, I just…wanted to talk to you."

"Clara, I love you, but please don't call me anymore. I can't handle it. Do you know I've been in therapy for the past four months? Therapy, Clara!"

"Why are you in therapy?"

"Because of you!" she yelled and I had to inch the phone away from my eardrum. "You blamed me for your parents' death. Do you know what that did to me?"

What the… Was she really turning the tragedy of the death of my parents around for me to feel sorry for her?

"I never blamed you, Addy. You're the one who brought that up. I never, ever said that I blamed you. We went out to a movie, there's nothing wrong with that. If I hadn't been gone with you I'd probably be dead, too."

"Oh! So now you're suicidal? You wanted to die with your parents and I denied you that?" she yelled and once again I had to pull the phone back.

"What is wrong with you? Why are you doing this? I just wanted to talk to my friend, about a guy."

"Well, I'm not your friend anymore, Clara, I can't be. It's too hard for me to hear your voice and know that we can never be friends like before."

"Why can't we? I wouldn't have called you if I didn't want to talk to you."

"Please call Dee or someone else when you feel the need to unload on someone."

Then she hung up.

It was the last straw, the final blow, the thingy that broke the camel's back. The tears flowed and the sob raised and I bawled into my pillow. I hadn't felt this abandoned and alone since my parents died. And I had absolutely no one to talk to about it.

But then, Eli was there. I knew he had dragged me into a Reverie and I tried to drag myself out. I pulled my eyelids up, but I couldn't be rid of it. I looked around and saw it was blank. We were nowhere. It was all white and nothing else.

"I thought I'd cheer you up by letting you pick the place," he explained behind me. I turned to look at him. "Ah, Clara," he said, seeing my state. His face fell. "I'm so sorry. I have so much to explain."

"I don't really want to hear it," I answered quietly without any real fire.

"I need you to," he insisted. "You believe something that is a complete lie."

"Eli, please don't. Why do you feel like you have to torture me?"

"I'm not," he assured and came close. He put his hands on the tops of my arms and spoke low. "Pick a place, anywhere you want."

My mind immediately went to the night we'd spent in Pastor's car at the docks. My cheeks burned at the memory and the fact that he knew why I chose this spot. I squeezed my eyes shut in frustration.

"Don't be embarrassed. I love this place, too."

"Eli, what do you want?" I pulled from his grasp and went to stand at the edge, looking over the water. "I don't think I can take much more tonight."

"I need you to understand something."

"What's that?"

"That you are the most important person there is for me and I have never loved nor wanted anyone before I met you."

"So," I turned to look at him, "you were just going to marry her and not love her?"

"Don't you remember what I said about our kind?" he answered slowly and came forward. "We don't love. Angelina doesn't love me," he said and I hated her name coming out of his mouth. I grit my teeth. He huffed and rubbed his neck. "Sorry." I shrugged so he went on. "I don't love her. She doesn't love me. It's a game. My parents orchestrated our marriage when we were born. She has always had some fantasy about it and when I left, it just made it worse. She finds it all a game to play and, like my brother, tracks me from city to city. Sometimes she finds me, sometimes she doesn't. Usually, I just head out of town as soon as I catch wind of her. But I have a dilemma this time."

"What?"

"You."

"Don't let me stop you," I said sulkily.

He inched closer. "I blanked at your house when you told me, and for that I'm sorry. I know what it must have looked like to you to say that to me and for me to not respond." He inched even closer. "But I was so shocked that she'd found me so quickly. My brother must have tipped her off. And that she had talked to you... It wouldn't be wise to provoke her and the idea of her speaking to you when I wasn't there…made me sick with worry for you." He inched the final inch. I was shivering in the cold, my arms crossed over my chest. Eli put his arms around me and slowly pulled me to him. He sighed when he realized I wasn't going to fight him. It was as if my arms uncrossed themselves and wound around him. He looked down into my face. "Clara…you have to know how I feel about you by now. I'd never, ever do anything to hurt you. The very thought of you in harms way makes *me* hurt. Please. I need you to believe me. Angelina is a hellish witch who cares for no one and nothing. Her sole want of me is to carry on our race and make her parents proud."

"But what about the other one? They both lied? That's what you're saying?"

"Ah," he said in understanding. "You must have also met my sister. Mara and Angelina travel together sometimes. She's equally as unpleasant. I'm so sorry. I hoped we'd have more time before my past came to catch up with us."

"Are you leaving?" I asked and was very unhappy with that thought. Even though I was still processing everything he was telling me.

"No," he said vehemently. "Why do you always jump to the conclusion that I'm about to skip town?"

"Because I..." I sighed and pulled back some, twisting my ring. "I don't..."

"I am not Tate," he insisted. "Tate was an idiot who took for granted what he had. I have no intentions of doing that. That is, if you'll still have me."

"I don't know. I'm so tired, Eli. I'm tired of feeling like I can't trust anyone anymore."

"You can trust me," he said softly. "Tell me what I can do? I need to earn your trust, Clara. I want to."

"I don't know what you can do. I'm scared."

"I know," he said knowingly and I looked up to his face to see him. He was holding it back, but I saw how hard he was straining. "Everything will be ok."

"How?"

"Because I'm here and I'm not going to leave you. I could have left a hundred times already. I could have just used you and been on my way. I could have just left after Angelina and my sister showed up. But I'm here," he insisted. "I'm here because I need to make sure you're ok and safe. I *want you*, Clara."

He was right. Why go through all this trouble? Why put up with my ex and come talk to me if there was a chance he could leave? He wanted to be here. I turned my ring and looked at him. Could he be the guy my mom always told me about? A guy who loved me and would do anything for me? Who loved me for me?

He saw me rubbing my ring and moved my fingers away as he took over. His thumb caressed it lovingly and I felt my anger melting away.

"I'm not going anywhere. Even if you won't have me, I'll still be here to make sure you're safe–"

I cut off his response with a swift hug around his neck. He pulled me up off the ground and held me tightly.

"I want you to stay."

"You believe me?" he asked quietly.

"Yes," I breathed. "This is going to sound very cheesy, but please don't hurt me. I don't think I can take anymore heartache right now."

"You have nothing to worry about on that front," he promised and put me down gently. He took my face in his hands. For a few seconds we just stared at each other with silent understanding. We were announcing that we were together, a couple, in for the long haul, we were defining the relationship. I pushed up on my tip toes to kiss him quickly and was awed at how right it all felt. It was like my body knew something I didn't. He pulled back slightly. "I've been given a gift, a chance at a new life with you. There's nothing in the world worth risking that."

I nodded and smiled when he laced both our hands together. His fingers lovingly caressing mine.

"I'm sorry," I said. "I wish I had let you explain before, but…your sister and …the other one were very convincing."

"That's what they're made to be like," he replied. I nodded again and yawned. He smiled sadly. "I'll take you home so you can sleep."

I felt a spike of unease about that. The thought of Eli alone, or me alone for that matter, was unnerving after everything that happened. Eli's grip tightened on mine and I watched him closely.

"Does it ever get easier for you?"

"I don't know. I've never felt positive emotion before. Your negative emotions affect me just like everybody else's, but your positive emotions have ten times the effect on me."

"Is that normal?"

"Yes," he said cautiously, "but, usually when we pair up with someone, they are…" he looked uncomfortable, "the mates are…they're evil, like us. The Devourer feeds off the despair and hatred of a human who matches their own and it makes them all the more powerful because they are never starved. I've never heard of a Devourer feeling positive emotion before. It seems you and I are one of a kind."

I smiled despite what he had just said. The end part was pretty good.

"I kind of like that," I mused softly.

"Me, too," he said against my forehead. "Home," he said and then I was standing in my bedroom again.

Eleven

After Eli left, I sat on my bed and contemplated the day. It was only about six o'clock by this point. Eli had promised that he'd come over, as planned, tonight for dinner. He left me so I could take a nap and think about everything that had happened. I was thinking alright...

About his tongue ring.

Was that shallow? After everything that happened I couldn't get the feel of his tongue ring - a smooth little silver ball - as it moved against my tongue and lips, out of my head.

When he'd dropped me off in my room, he had kissed me for a very long time. He'd been afraid that I was done with him and needed assurance that I truly believed him and was going to wade through the craziness to make this work.

If I was completely honest, I was scared myself. I didn't know what his sister and Angelina were up to or how to get rid of them. I didn't know what to do about his brother either, but Eli assured me that he had no intentions of leaving me. We'd work this out somehow, and then he had kissed me silly. His hands on my lower back pressed and pulled to bring me close as I gripped his upper arms. When he had finally pulled back he said, "Do you feel that?"

I had no idea what he was talking about, but he swiftly said his goodbyes and promised to see me in a couple hours.

I lay back on the bed and closed my eyes to accept the darkness. I knew I'd be alone when I closed my eyes and that was ok. If Eli was going to be coming to me and taking me to places when I closed my eyes at night, I'd have to start learning to take a nap or two.

~ ~ ~

The doorbell woke me. I jolted up and glanced in the mirror, smoothing my hair. I ran down the hall and stopped to take a calming breath - so it didn't look like I'd just ran down the hall - and opened the door to find Eli with a little sly grin. I bit my lip and started to return it but once again I just knew.

"Enoch," I said angrily. "What are you doing at my house?" I tried to keep calm. Knowing he could literally feel and taste my fear made it that much worse.

"So it's true," he said in an angry awe and came a little closer as if examining me. "I can feel it."

"Feel what? What are you talking about?"

"You're bonded with him." He gazed at something between us with disgust. I watched him curiously.

"With Eli? What?" Enoch came even closer to completely invade my space. I sucked in a quick breath and he groaned slightly. "I'm not going to hurt you, silly. I couldn't even if I wanted to. You don't see this?"

He motioned between us. I looked and saw nothing but air and space. I looked at him questioningly.

"When we mate-" he started, but was interrupted by Mrs. Ruth.

"Eli! Nice to see you again." She glanced between us. "Well, let him in, Clara, don't just stand in the door, honey."

"No," I said quickly, "this isn't Eli."

She raised her eyebrow and gave me an amusing look. "Ok," she said sarcastically. "Eli, come on in. Dinner's almost ready."

"No really, this is Enoch, Eli's twin."

"Oh," she said and looked closer to him. "Identical. Wow, I'd have never known. How nice that you came, too. I'm sure we have plenty if you want to stay for dinner." She held out her hand to him. "Ruth, the Pastor's wife."

"Enoch," he said smoothly and took her hand, bringing it to his lips, before I could stop him, and kissing it. "Pleasure," he rumbled.

Her face flamed a shade between red and pink. "Oh," she whispered. "Um."

I pulled her hand free and glared at him.

"He's not staying," I assured her. "He just came by to say farewell as he skipped out of town. Isn't that right, Enoch?"

"Well, it doesn't look like there's much fun to be had here anymore," he explained flatly.

"Goodbye, then. Safe travels," Mrs. Ruth said briskly before turning to go back to the kitchen.

"What is wrong with you?" I hissed at him.

"Evil being," he said and pointed to himself. "If that's not an excuse, I don't know what is."

"There's no excuse for being a jerk."

"But she's the Pastor's wife… Do you not understand the irony of this whole situation?" he said clearly enjoying himself. "One evil being at your door, kissing the hand of your adopted mother who's married to the Pastor with whom you live. You, the sweet, innocent, unscathed mate of my twin brother who renounces what he is, but is also…an evil being. I mean, you can't write this stuff."

"Just get out of here," I said and tried to shut the door.

"'Fraid I can't do that, love," he said sweetly as his hand snapped out swiftly to hold the door open.

"Don't call me that."

"But you're family now," he said sarcastically and jerked me forward with a hand on my wrist. He pulled me out the door and pushed me against the house side, my wrist still in his surprisingly gentle grasp. "Don't you understand what I've been trying to tell you?"

"No, I don't." I tried to pull away, but he held tight. "You're hurting me."

"No, I'm not." He grinned and inched forward. His face was almost touching mine and I held my breath. "You little liar," he breathed and I felt it wash against my lips.

It was true, he wasn't hurting me, but I wasn't comfortable like this either.

"Let me go," I commanded in a whisper.

"Not until you hear what I have to say."

"What?" I said in exasperated annoyance. "What do you have to say?"

"That you're in trouble," he said low and foreboding.

Before I could speak I heard a growl off to the side. We both looked in that direction to see Eli. I wasn't surprised to see him. He'd told me he was coming over, but I was surprised to see his face at least a shade too red to be normal and the veins in his neck and arms were blue. Yes, blue and bulging. He shook with rage and I felt a second's spike of fear as he speared his brother with a glare.

His gaze immediately shot to mine and he visibly calmed; his veins seemed to be less prominent and his fist shook less as he heaved a long breath.

"Don't be scared of me, Clara," he said gruffly.

"Have you looked at yourself, brother?" Enoch chimed happily, but didn't release me nor back away. "I haven't seen you this enraged since I stole that girl from you in Philadelphia."

"That was over a hundred years ago and I was stupid back then. I am not the same, as it seems to so easily escape your grasp, brother," he spat.

"I'm not the only one who lets things slip their grasp." He leaned back a little, but held me firmly to the wall. Eli's eyes shifted to the space between us and his eyes widened to impossible half dollars. Then his gaze settled on me.

Anyone else would have been frightened out of their mind. But you see, the look on Eli's face was something indescribable. The way he felt for me, the affection, the care, the...love, was all over him as if I could see it written in ink there.

"Clara," he said, his voice was almost a beg.

I didn't understand what was going on, but I wasn't scared of it either. Enoch interrupted anything that was going on between us.

"You see?" He turned to look at me again and sneered. "I couldn't hurt her even if I wanted to. So you can relax, little girl."

"What are you talking about?" I asked in a harsh whisper.

"You don't see that?" Eli asked.

"See what?"

"Come here, Clara. Enoch, let her go."

Enoch's hand gently released my wrist and he backed away. I made a swift move to Eli who had completely returned to himself. He was no longer filled with rage, and his eyes never left my face.

I let my fingers hover over the skin of his neck over a vein, plump it pumped his blood, but was invisible now. I asked the silent question with my eyes as I took my hand away.

"Forgive me for that. I didn't mean to frighten you."

"What was that?"

"It was protection," Enoch said across the porch. "He thought I was hurting you."

I ignored him. "What do you see that I don't see?" I asked Eli.

"We're bound," he said, barely a whisper, in fact I really just read his lips.

"What does that mean," I asked in the same fashion.

"It means that Enoch is correct. He can not hurt you…because he, too, is bound to you."

"I don't understand."

"There's a string…" His fingers moved between us into clear air and nothingness. "Why can't you see it?"

"A string?"

"There's a barbed strand here…between you and I and between you…and Enoch."

I gulped. I glanced at Enoch and he was stoically watching me. He didn't look like he was surprised so he'd apparently already seen it. I looked back to Eli. He touched my face softly, almost as if seeing if I was real. I heard Enoch tell him, "No, don't," but I didn't understand why. Then my gaze snapped alive with a new brightness.

Although it was darker I could see better than before. Like it wasn't dark, but a bright sunny day. The colors of Eli's white shirt and black button up and the grass below us was contrasted to high definition levels. But most importantly, I saw the string attached around my wrist and his. It was black and barbed as he said, like it hooked into us like barbed wire, taut and ridged, but I didn't feel anything. It had a haze around it and the ethereal look of it made it seem smoky and unfocused.

His fingers barely caressed my cheek and then slid down my neck and arm. When he looked back up his face changed. He tilted his head to look more closely into my eyes. His jaw dropped slightly and a stunned breath blew across my face.

"I told you to stop," Enoch said behind us. "Idiot."

"What?" I said confused. I felt a prickle of unease shoot through me that whatever he was going to say wouldn't be something I'd be thrilled about.

"My eyes."

"What about them?"

"Your…I completely forgot. Your eyes…are like mine now."

"What do you mean?" My heart pounded. "They're purple?"

"No, they're green, but you can see like me. When I touched you I gave you my perspective. The green is just a backlash, some kind of mishap or something. We have no idea why they turn green instead of purple, but it happens when the two bound ones touch for the first time. You noticed the sight?"

"Yes," I answered and looked around again, "everything is brighter and more focused."

"How are we going to explain this to your guardians?" he mused more to himself.

"Wait," I asked in my most calm voice. "My eyes are really green? Really?"

"Yes," he nodded solemnly, "and they'll stay that way."

I wanted to panic and I wanted to do…something. But I knew my reaction was important right now. The way Eli viewed me and handled me from now on hinged on my reaction to this moment; my reaction to something supernatural and awe inspiring happening to us. We were bound somehow. And that part of the equation thrilled me. It was the other stuff that was making me want to bolt. I thought long and hard about my next statement. One, to make sure I wasn't lying to him and the words were true and two, to make sure my voice was calm before I said them.

"Well…I'll tell them I got contacts or something. I'll tell them I was tired of blue," I tried to come to a solution when really, weirdly, strangely, I found it oddly satisfying that I was in possession of something that only Eli could give me; his view of the world.

It hadn't really hit me that this might change my world entirely. It scathed by my thoughts that things may be different in every way but Eli seemed to function, so could I, right?

"Maybe," he thought, "but they are *really* green, Clara. In the mean time, put these on." He took the aviator glasses hanging on his shirt collar and put them on me. I grimaced and wrinkled my nose. "What?" he asked me, his lip twitching as it fought a smile.

"Aviators are so not my style."

He laughed and smoothed my hair before saying, "Please try not to be such a girl right now."

"I am a girl," I countered.

"A girl who looks fine in my sunglasses," he insisted with a little smirk. "Besides, we have bigger things to worry about."

I looked back down between us to see the barb connecting our wrists and looked back up to Eli's face.

"What does this mean? What is this?"

"It's a linkage," he explained in a soft voice. "A bond."

"Like what you were talking about before? Because I'm your…mate?"

"Not quite," he answered carefully.

"Tell her, brother," Enoch said snidely. "Tell her what it means."

"Shut up." He looked at me closely and carefully. His face was lit with a glow I'd never seen before. He almost smiled. "Later," he promised in a low rumble.

"Why not now?" I insisted. "I'm not exactly known for my patience."

Enoch laughed, "Oh, we can see that."

"Shut up," Eli told him again and looked back to me. "I will explain, but not right now. Besides..." He stepped back and stuck his hands in his pockets. "Pastor, good to see you again."

Pastor had just turned the corner and look up startled.

"Oh, Eli, hello. And..." He looked at Enoch with a hilarious expression. "Eli?"

I giggled nervously and both Eli and Enoch chuckled.

"This is Eli's brother, Enoch," I told him.

"Nice to meet you, Preach," Enoch stated and shook his hand. "I'm just visiting my little brother here from out of town."

"I thought you were twins?"

"We are. But I was born first."

"By 6 minutes and he never lets me forget it," Eli offered. He extended his hand, too, and smiled. "Good to see you again, sir."

"You, too, son. You staying for dinner?"

"If the Mrs. will have me."

"I'm sure she will. Enoch?"

I started to butt in and state that he was absolutely not staying, but he declined. "Nah. I'm on a strict diet, but thanks anyway."

"Ok," Pastor said easily, but quirked a brow at him. "Do you mind if I ask where you're from? Your accent is more pronounced than Eli's. Where did you boys grow up?"

"Amsterdam," Enoch answered while Eli said, "Africa."

Eli laughed and then said, "We moved around a lot, lived all over. I guess that's why our accents are hard to place."

"Huh," Pastor said. "Well, good to meet you, Enoch."

"And you as well," he answered slowly.

Pastor turned to look at me and cocked his head, looking thoroughly amused. "Sunglasses at night? Do I want to ask?"

"I wouldn't, Pastor," I said grinning, trying to deflect. "It's a Diva thing."

He laughed and nodded. As soon as he went inside I turned to stare at both of them.

"Answers," I demanded.

"All in good time, princess," Enoch said grinning. "You need to enjoy your family dinner and I need to…trick some silly girl into feeding me. We'll meet somewhere tonight and discuss it all."

I groaned and turned away, disgusted. Eli grasped my fingers and I looked at the barbed string connecting us all. I turned back to the door. Although I was in awe of the whole situation, I didn't want to think about how Enoch got his kicks.

"Get out of here," Eli told him. I heard footsteps retreating and then Eli's arms came around me from behind. "I'm sorry."

There was so much in his sorry; hurt, love, trust…regret. I turned in his arms and looked at him. What was he sorry for? As if he read my mind he answered me.

"I'm sorry for dragging you into my world."

"I'm not exactly kicking and screaming," I said coyly.

He didn't laugh at my joke. He lifted my hand and placed it to his cheek. He inhaled the skin at my wrist and rubbed his scruffy chin on my palm. He then kissed it and held on to me as he pulled me inside to have dinner with my family without another word.

Twelve

"I'm sorry you're not feeling well. We could have done this another time, Clara," Mrs. Ruth said in response to my 'migraine' excuse for wearing sunglasses at the dinner table.

"It's ok, it's not too bad, I just wanted to head it off, you know?" I explained and she nodded.

"So, Eli, where are you planning to go to school?" she asked him as she spoon fed one of the babies.

"I'm not sure, to be honest. I've thought about moving away somewhere. Like Colorado or something."

"What's in Colorado? A certain school you'd like to go to?"

"Well…I actually already took my core college classes, I just need to figure out my major. I'm just not sure what I want to do yet, but I'd love to live somewhere really secluded. Maybe finish college online."

"Ahh. Well, Clara would miss you," she said with certainty. Eli and just looked at each other over our rice pilaf.

"Well," Pastor replied, "I for one think it's commendable that you've got a head start on college. Clara, it would seem, isn't all that interested," he said, stating facts.

"I'm a little confused right now…on what I want to do and what my parents wanted me to do," I muttered. I hadn't even realized I'd said it out loud until I felt Mrs. Ruth's hand on mine. I glanced up to see everyone staring at me in understanding. "Sorry."

"Don't be sorry," she said and patted my hand. "And don't worry about the dishes. You guys go on and do something, I'll get them."

"Would it be alright if I took Clara to the park for a bit?" Eli asked cautiously.

"Sure," Pastor said easily, "as long as you bring her home-"

"By midnight," I answered for him and laughed as I grabbed Eli's hand to drag him with me. "I know."

"Have fun, kids, and be careful."

"We will," I called and shut the door. I didn't bother to grab anything. "So," I started, "we're meeting your jerk of a brother at the park?"

"Yep."

"Did you text him or something? How do you know that?""

"We're family. We can call each other in our minds but I've been blocking them all out for years. I opened up and told him where."

He grabbed my hand after we crossed the four lane.

"So, you see this way all the time?" I asked as I squinted at the streetlights. "It's strange. It's not like night vision, it's just…bright." I again felt a tick of nervousness as having to see this way all the time. What would things look like in the day time? What was I going to do about my green eyes, that I hadn't even seen myself yet?

"It's ok," he assured me and squeezed my fingers, "it's normal."

"I think we are well past the realm of normal, Eli," I muttered even as I continued to take in my surroundings. The string between us was particularly interesting. I copied his earlier movements and wrapped my fingers around it, almost expecting it to cut me with its sharp looking barbs. It floated between my fingers and my palm and it seemed to flex and move with me, like I was a part of it. Or it was a part of me. I couldn't feel it between my fingers and it didn't make any sense.

I pulled him to a stop.

"Please tell me what this means," I said on a voice that left no more room for stalling. He nodded.

"I want to explain it to you before Enoch shows up anyway."

"Ok," I edged.

"This," he moved his fingers along the string, "means that we're bonded."

"And that's different than just being your mate?"

"Yes," he said quietly. "When we choose a mate, that's exactly what it is. We feel a connection with you and choose to keep you and you don't really have much say. Yes, you feel strange around us and you feel connected but other than that, technically you could walk away and be fine if we let you. But this…this linkage is a decision, Clara."

"A decision? What…you decided to bond yourself to me?"

"No, Clara." He paused for an agonizing dramatic affect. "You did."

"What?" I said in my stunned high voice. "How could I have known? I don't even know what you're saying."

"I'm saying," he said softly and pulled me to him. His hands held my waist loosely, as if he was telling me he wanted to touch me but wasn't holding me against my will. I could leave when I wanted. "You may not have realized what it meant, but somehow, you made the decision subconsciously…that you wanted to keep me."

Even though this was Eli, even though we knew there was more between us than some lame crush, I still flushed at his implication. I saw his smile as he gazed at me, but oddly he didn't flinch or gasp as he registered my emotion. And his smile was genuine, not cocky, not smug. I swallowed hard and took a deep breath, my hands made their way to his upper arms.

"So you're saying that this is my fault," I said and motioned between us. "I don't understand how this is different from the mating thing."

"When we mate, like I said, it's something that happens to us both but ultimately, it's almost slavery. They really shouldn't even call it a mate because it's anything but romantic. A consort is more like it. The Devourer owns them, carts them everywhere, parades them around. The mate just stays because of the strange feelings they have for the Devourer. And most of them are shady and don't mind the protection and lifestyle they get from us."

"So," I thought carefully, "that's what I'm going to be? Just following you around everywhere like a puppy?"

"No. Of course not."

"But before this you said I was your mate. What were you going to do with me?" I asked, not unkindly.

"I wasn't sure. I had no plans to use you if that's what you mean."

"I just meant…I don't know what I mean," I sighed and looked at the ground between us. "I just don't know how to take all this. You're telling me that I chose this, wanted this. But I don't see how that's possible when I didn't know it was something I *could* do."

"It doesn't matter." He smiled a brilliantly bright and happy smile. "Do you have any idea what it means, that you did this. I can keep you safe now, my family has no choice but to protect you. I won't need anything but you for the rest of my life to sustain me."

I got his meaning and it thrilled me in an odd way.

"Is that why you aren't freaking out and breathing funny?"

He chuckled.

"Yes." He laughed again. "Yes, that's why. The bond gives me everything I need. I'll only actually feel it when you have a sudden or intense spike of emotion." He leaned forward and kissed the corner of my mouth. I sucked in a quick breath and he laughed before he groaned slightly. "Like that."

I allowed him to pull me up to him and kiss me. He moved with surety and conviction, like there was nothing else to do in the moment. As he held me, I felt something in my world crack. I realized that I should be completely freaking out. Completely.

This guy I'd only known for a few short weeks had somehow convinced me that I'd bound myself to him, literally, with an invisible barbed connection from my wrist to his. My life in the past few days seemed to have been flushed down the toilet in a un-ceremonial kind of way and then lifted up again by someone who could only be described as a bad guy turned good.

It wasn't the first time I'd thought about what my parents would think of my dating him. I had so many questions that my head hurt to even begin to organize them. But in the turmoil of my internal tirade I'd come to one conclusion: somehow, this guy who seemed to know me, who cared about me, who was intensely enjoying my lips right now, had saved me.

Saved me from what, you say? I had an ok life, you say? I was spoiled and privileged and had everything most people wanted and could never have, you say?

True to all accounts except for one minor thing and in my book the most important thing. I wasn't free.

I had been trapped; in my life, my memories, my friends, my guilt, my need to be what everyone else wanted me to. No one could save me from that life. No one but someone on the outside who saw me for who I was and not what everyone else had painted me to be.

Eli saved me from myself. I had every intention of taking advantage of it and figuring out exactly who I wanted to be from this day on.

He interrupted anything else I may have thought or said by pulling slightly away and looking down into my face.

"Wait..." He stepped back and I knew nothing good would come from that act. "Wait. No, this is wrong."

"What?" I asked confused.

"I could no sooner ask you to do this than I could ask you ask you to run away with me."

That idea actually sounded kind of appealing but I jerked back to attention as he went on.

"You don't know what you're doing," he said in a voice that was like boxes being dragged on concrete. "You were right, you had no idea and somehow did this haphazardly. I'm sorry, I can't tell how sorry I am to have dragged you into all this. I'll find a way - a way to release you-"

"What are you talking about?" Talk about an about-face. "Where did all that come from? I thought you were happy about this?"

"Clara, it's too much. I couldn't ask it of you."

"I didn't ask you to. I'm offering."

"Don't," he ground out. "Don't tempt me to just take you. I can't do that. You have a life here, a way of living that suits you. I'm just a passing distraction, a phase. You'll forget about me one day and be ok."

"I hate this part," I sighed in aggravation and jerked the sunglasses from my eyes, setting them atop my head into my hair.

"What?" he said in a voice that clearly didn't understand where I could be leading things.

"This is where the leading man tries to save the girl from herself. She is willing to give up everything for him and he, in his misguided attempt to save her, tells her he's skipping for the hills and she has to beg him to stay and convince him that her love is real and that she is sound of mind."

He watched me and took a small step towards me even as he tilted his head a little.

"Love?" he whispered.

Had I said that? Yikes. I ignored that he'd said that at all and continued on.

"Furthermore, I think it's juvenile to assume that just because a girl makes a romantic gesture that she can't possibly know what's in her own head." He moved even closer, but I kept my gaze on the top button of his shirt. I felt a little loony, but the words kept spewing out. "I didn't exactly have a great life here, you knew that, and for you to just assume like you could come in here and alter everything I knew like this and then just leave is-" My breath caught as he made that last inch between us non-existent. "It's just cruel. I mean, you gave me these green eyes, you made me want you and then you want to just-"

He pulled my face up to look into his, but I kept my eyes away. He sat silently until I caved and directed my gaze to his. When I took in the amount of gratitude and - oh, I must be imagining the rest – I shivered in response.

He didn't say anything, just snaked an arm around my back and held me tightly as he looked at me for several long, loaded seconds. Then he bent his head and let his lips skim my forehead. "I hope you know what you're doing."

"I know what I want," I answered in rebuttal.

"Why don't you let me lay it all out for you?" He pulled back to look at me. "My world is…dangerous, crazy, it never sleeps. You may want no part in it when you know exactly what comes in the whole package."

"I'm so glad we're back to treating me like some ditsy damsel in distress that can't decide what's good for her," I said sulkily.

He chuckled at me, which in any other circumstance might have made me mad, but right then, I was just trying to figure out why he wanted me to say 'no' so badly.

"Clara," he sighed my name. "Ok," he gave in, "I'll let you decide for yourself, but just let it be said when you hate me one day that I tried to warn you."

His words were harsh, but his expression was solemn and deciding.

"I could never hate you, Eli. And I may not know everything about your world and the people who we'll meet along the way, but I'm graduating soon and I have no intentions of staying in this town. I want to…go everywhere, see everything. I want to go with you anywhere you'll take me…and I want you to *want* to take me with you."

"I do," he said roughly and let his fingers move across my chin. "I want you. This isn't about not wanting you. It's about keeping you safe and you not regretting your life."

"Then trust me. I think the safest place for me is with you, and I won't regret it. I don't regret anything. The things that we do and the things that happen…to us," I gulped and pushed down memories, "make us who we are."

"You are a fascinating, breathtaking creature, CB. I hope you understand that to the fullest."

"I do," I said coyly and he cracked a smile. A real smile that was genuine and in no way to appease me.

"Last time I'll ask and then I'm done. You're sure you want this? You're sure that I'm worth this?"

"No question. I think…" I felt the answer to one of my earlier internal questions come flitting to me and I rubbed my promise ring, "if my mom were here, she would have loved you."

"You have no idea what you've done for me," he said and his face twisted into an anguished expression. His hands on my sides squeezed a little and it hurt to see him so upset. "I've spent my whole life being a…parasite. I never wanted this, Clara," he said in a vehement beg. "Do you understand? I never wanted to be what I am."

My breathing took ragged steps to work properly as I tried to comfort him by saying, "I know. But Eli, you're not the same person anymore."

"Because of you," he said with a conviction that rumbled into my bones. "I won't ever feed again from anyone. You've given me a gift beyond what I can imagine. I'll never have to hurt anyone to survive again. I'll be able to live normally and be myself with no fear of my nature taking me over. I'll be free," he mused and I smiled in understanding and nodded my head, but he continued. "You saved me from being the monster I *could have* been."

We were both free now and the impact of everything he said hit me like a piano from the second floor.

"I didn't mean to upset you," he said softly as he wiped under my eye. "I was harsh."

"No, dummy. They're tears of happiness."

"Then, I'm honored," he said quietly.

I smiled and hugged him tighter, my wet cheek resting on his chest. His warm arms encircled me once more and he kneaded my body with them, as if to assure and comfort me. He pressed and moved and I felt him kiss my hair. We stayed like that, content in our own thinking processes of what was happening.

And then the jerk who shared my guy's face came and decided to grace us with his presence.

"Gross," he muttered behind us. "If I'm going to have to bear witness to this every day, just kill me now."

Thirteen

"Buzz off," Eli said in dismissal and to my enjoyment and chagrin, he pulled my face up and planted a kiss on me that melted bones and forewent apology.

"Oh, bother," Enoch groaned. "He's told you already hasn't he?"

"Yes," Eli answered against my lips and pulled back to grasp my hand instead. "It seems we didn't need your expertise after all," he said sarcastically.

"Oh, this is not over," Enoch promised and came forward looking menacing and every bit of upset and angry as his fist hardened at his sides. "I thought you were going to try to talk her into letting you go."

"What?" I looked at Eli accusingly. "You told him about that? I thought you just decided that when-"

"Clara," Eli chided and smoothed my hair, "I have no idea what my idiot brother is talking about."

"Standing right here," Enoch muttered and crossed his arms. I noticed his eyebrow ring was gone now. Huh. "Look, I didn't need you to tell me. I knew you, the selfless hero, would try to save her from her own stupidity and lack of self preservation."

"That's what I said," I muttered under my breath, "only without the last part."

"What?" Enoch hissed at me.

"We should talk, yes," Eli agreed. "Let's go into the park and find a spot."

"You two are idiotic. I hope you know that," Enoch muttered as he led the way through the grass. It crunched under our feet and the night air had turned a little chilly. I regretted not wearing sleeves.

"Just shut up," Eli answered him.

"This is not going to fly and you know it." He turned to glare at us both, his gaze lingering on me a little longer than Eli. "You know what our kind will say, and to drag the feeler into it is just...cruel."

Feeler?

"You care, brother?" Eli asked and smiled cockily.

"You can see the string just as easily as I can. I don't want to care about her!" he yelled and came to stand in front of Eli with a swiftness that startled me. "I wasn't made for this. I was not made to want to protect," he looked down at me with disdain, "human girls, just use them."

"Enoch," Eli growled in warning.

"And for the record, this is by far the stupidest thing I've witnessed by you, brother. Her, I can see, but you? "

I stayed quiet, though I wanted to say something in retaliation.

"I didn't choose this, but I wouldn't change it," Eli explained. "I know we have a rough road ahead, but I fully intend to avoid our kind at all costs. I know you weren't made for this and it rubs you the wrong way to feel something for her," Enoch let out a guttural retort to that, "but the thing is, you don't have to like Clara. You just have to protect her."

"Wait," I could hold off no longer as my gaze latched onto the barbed string connecting my wrist to Enoch's, "I don't understand. Why does he have to protect me? Are we in trouble? Is your kind not supposed to..." I motioned between us to the string, "do this? Be connected like this?"

"They're no rules. It's not that we're not supposed to, it just doesn't happen very often," Eli explained and rubbed my knuckles with his thumb. "It makes the others think the Devourer has gone soft. They think we'll want to change the way things are for everyone. Like I told you, usually it's a slavery type situation and though the mate may enjoy it - all the parties and the wild lifestyle - they don't...love their Devourer."

My cheeks burned. I pressed on.

"So why does Enoch need to protect me?"

"When one of us has a linkage with our mate, it means something a little different. Because my family is bound to you too, they will feel the need to protect you as well."

"But we don't have to like you," Enoch made sure to point out.

"Your family is linked to me," I repeated. "I'm bonded to your family. Does that mean you can all read my thoughts or something?"

"No," Eli laughed, "it doesn't really mean anything to you. You won't ever feel anything from it, and neither will they except if you're in danger. It sounds complicated but really, it's not. It's simple." He pulled me to him again. "You chose me, Clara, and I chose you. End of story."

"Bloody hell," Enoch muttered as I looked into Eli's fathomless violets. "I'm out of here."

"Where are you going?" Eli asked, keeping his eyes on mine.

"Away."

"But we still haven't discussed Angelina," he told him and finally looked away from me to glare at Enoch. "Low blow, brother."

"Well," he gloated, "I thought your life here could use a little spice."

"You brought her here?" I asked and accepted his hard stare with as much courage as I could muster.

"If it's any consolation, it was before you were bound," he said and smiled cruelly. "Man, I'd love to see a cat fight between you two. Though it wouldn't last long," he waged and shook his head thoughtfully.

"Enoch," Eli barked, "I swear if you don't stop I'll–"

"You'll what, brother? Behead me like they tried to do in Italy, or run with through with spikes like in Rome? Since you don't remember, apparently, I'll remind you; I can't be killed, just as you can't. So spare me your pathetic threats. It's demeaning to our kind to watch you play human."

"Don't toy with us. Be on your way and leave us alone, but don't play these games and invite trouble where there doesn't have to be any."

"Where's the fun in that?"

"Everything isn't about fun!" Eli yelled and even in the darkness and dim streetlights I saw the veins in his arms begin to bulge a hue of dark blue. "Sometimes things are serious and need to be handled as such. You're a fool if you think that this can be settled with a little fight. This will cause problems all the way around if you don't stop meddling. Angelina won't take this lightly and you, being that you're tied to Clara now, will have no choice but to help in the cause. Fitting, sense you caused all this to begin with."

"I'm done," Enoch said harshly. "I didn't sign up for any of this. I'm going to go somewhere far away. Somewhere anywhere but here."

I thought Eli would try to say something, stop his brother who was clearly upset by all this. He didn't. So I did. Little did I know it was a huge mistake.

"I'm sorry, Enoch. I didn't realize-"

"Don't," he sneered. "You really think I want your pity?"

"I just thought…I didn't mean for this to happen. I had no control-"

"Just stop talking," he growled and took a step towards us.

"Watch it, Enoch," Eli boomed beside me.

"What? You may not claim to be one anymore, brother, but I do. I am a Devourer! We don't care if little girls are scared, in fact we revel in it. I can't stay here, don't you understand? I don't care if something happened to make it this way between us all, I'm not sticking around to see the outcome. I don't care if your human is happy or safe, ok? And it shames me to my core that you do."

I'd never had that amount of poison directed at me before except from Deidre and even then, it was popsicles compared to this.

"It's probably best that you leave. Right now," Eli said carefully and I rubbed his arm where the veins threatened to burst.

"Gladly."

He marched away from us. We watched him go in silence that wasn't pregnant, but instead was waiting and patient. The sooner he left, the faster we could regroup and come up with a plan. But as he stepped into the pathway to weave between the bushes, I heard an 'oomph' before Enoch skidded in the dirt and grass in front of us ending at our feet.

We all looked up and the first thing I saw was long legs in skinny jeans as the moonlight skimmed its way up her body. Then a white blouse with a black bra. Then blazing red hair that was now cut into a seriously short shorn bob. Angelina. And she looked all too happy to be interrupting our little get together.

"Enoch, I think you should stay. We have much to…discuss…" her words faltered as she eyed the string from me to Enoch…and the one from me to Eli. Her pretty white face twisted into rage and hatred as the veins in her neck and forehead bulged and blazed blue like rivers and streams down her skin. She eyed me with clear intent. She was going to end me or go down trying.

"Angelina," Eli said easily and I still cringed at hearing him say her name. He glanced back for a split second and squeezed my hand before going on. "You know what this means. Just go home."

"Oh, I don't think I'll be doing that, darling," she said sweetly. "See, I thought Clara and I had an agreement. When I told her I was your fiancé she was supposed to run away, not bind herself to you." She glowered at Enoch, who hadn't gotten up from his crouch on the ground yet. "Gee, I wonder how she knew to do that?"

"Why are you looking at me?" Enoch growled before hopping up moving quickly off to the side. "I'm the one who called you, remember?"

"Yes, well, you are the one to always stir up trouble. Having fun yet?"

He sneered, "Oh yeah. Buckets and buckets." He dusted off his jeans for good measure.

"Leave," Eli called loudly. "Just leave. You can't do anything more here. You know that. The linkage is permanent."

"Well, I wonder what would happen to your bond if she were to perish?" Angelina mused and tapped her finger on her hip in contemplation.

I felt my breath leave me and waited for Eli to snap his arm around me, and he did, but the thing that surprised me was Enoch's arm around me too. I looked at him curiously and he looked at me. Then grimaced and took a step away.

"Bloody hell," he said and looked as if he'd be sick and then punch anyone around just for being there.

"What are you..." Angelina questioned. "Did you just..." She laughed humorlessly, a peel of ringing tones that grated my nerves. "I'm sorry, I'm just trying to process what I'm seeing. I could not have seen you attempt to save the feeler...from me?" she asked Enoch incredulously.

"You know how the bond works, Ang. Don't get sulky. I have no choice," Enoch replied sweetly.

"Don't call me Ang!" she screamed and even stomped her foot in the dirt.

I took all my power not to laugh at her. It literally hurt to hold it in.

"Fine, no Ang, but you know I'd never protect her unless I had a choice, which I've already stated that I clearly do not."

"You know I can take you, Enoch," she said with a little smile. "I was always better and faster than you. Come on, say it," she taunted.

"Sure, I'll agree with that, when I'm dead," he said steadily, but his veins gave him away. They began to bulge just as Eli's had.

"That can be arranged, Knocky," she said as an endearment but her actions were anything but. She charged him.

I froze in terror. There were really going to have a fight to the death in the park, right here in front front of us? Angelina and Enoch both glanced my way and licked their lips.

"Oh my," Angelina sang, "she tastes divine, Eli. I could almost forgive you for betraying me with her for that."

Enoch recovered more quickly and took that as his opportunity for a pot shot.

As I peeked around Eli's arm, I saw Enoch pick her up by one leg and one arm and toss her into the high pine trees. I heard crunches and thrashing branches and gripped Eli's arm tighter to hold in my scream. But him and Enoch both were still tense and on alert. Then I saw her…she was flying.

Or falling rather.

She fell from the sky as fast as a bullet and landed in a crouch on the ground in front of Enoch. She had jumped that high, I realized, and landed perfectly fine and cat-like. There were apparently more things that Eli hadn't told me about yet in regards to the things their kind could do.

"Nice try, but foul ball," she told Enoch and moved, too fast for my eyes to see, around to his back. She snapped his neck and he fell to the ground in a heap of awkward arms and legs.

I could no longer contain my scream. Eli clutched me to him and then placed me behind him completely when Angelina made her cat like strides our way.

"He's not dead, Clara. He's very much alive and will be madder than hornets when he awakens," he told me before turning back to her. "You've wasted so much time. You have chased me across every continent, state, and ocean. Don't you think it's time to let go of this? Find yourself a mate and be done with this game," he said to her and it strained with trying to keep it steady.

"Oh, Eli," she said softly. "You don't understand anything do you? After all this time, all the long years and many places we've been. All the people who know of our…situation, I can't just let you go. This isn't about having you for myself anymore, don't you see? I just can't lose. I refuse to lose face in front of my entire race because you had some freakish moral breakthrough years ago. Before that, you didn't seem to be so disgusted by my advances, as I recall." She smiled and I felt the blood drain from my face.

Were they together? Eli had said he'd never cared about nor loved her. I assumed that meant he'd never been with her…

"CB," he whispered. I looked up to find him watching my silent freak out. He shook his head a 'no'. "She's trying to plant the seed of doubt. Don't let her. I didn't lie, we were never together."

"Of course you would lie," she laughed. "What would you have to gain from telling her the truth?"

"Trust," Eli told her harshly as I gripped his arm, "something you'll never understand."

She sighed and came forward slowly, stepping over Enoch's body as if he were nothing.

"Elijah, it's not just about saving face," she said and put on a serious expression. "I miss you. I miss the way you used to be. Back then, you were feisty and I admired your rebellion of our union because it meant you wouldn't be told what to do. It was a clear sign of your leadership and kingship. I knew eventually you'd come around on your own terms one day and that we would be magnificent together. But then when I found you in Bangkok, and you told me that asinine story about the little feeler boy in the diner…I wondered then if you'd ever come back around. But you know what, I never gave up on you. And I'm not going to now."

"I don't need saving," he insisted in a hiss. "This is what I want."

"But you've been put under a spell," she replied and I almost believed her, she sounded so sincere, if it hadn't been for her carefully matriculated steps towards us. "Can't you see? That boy was a sorcerer of some sort. And her," she spat and glanced at me, "she's somehow found a way to bind you to her. That's the only reason you want to stay."

"I wanted her before she bound me. She was my mate. She's the reason I stayed in this town. I'm not budging, so you may as well get it through that arrogant head of yours that just because every other male on the planet may find you irresistible, doesn't make it true and doesn't mean that I have to."

Her lips twisted and turned, pursing into a frown. "That was almost a sweet thing to say. So we're at a stalemate, then? You won't give up your pride to come back with me and I won't give up mine to let you come back on your own. Hmmm."

"That's not what this is," he yelled. "Just leave!"

"But then who will direct the Horde when they finally get here?" she said and smiled in her knowledge that she had him. Whatever it was she was talking about apparently wasn't good.

Fourteen

"You summoned the Horde?" Eli asked incredulously. "How could you do that? You're not only damning me, you're damning my whole family."

"Yes," she said gleefully. "The price you pay for being a Thames just went up it seems."

"My sister… How could you do this to her? Your friend?"

"She won't know I did it until it's too late. Friends count under casualties of war." Her pretty face turned hateful once more and she boomed her words. "She'll pay for your crimes and it will be on your newfound conscience, Eli! This is all your fault! If only you'd given into me. Is it such a big thing to ask?"

"I'd rather burn in hell," he barked.

"Well, it looks like you'll get your chance."

Suddenly, Eli turned to me quickly and kissed my lips. I gasped at the quickness of it. Then we were somehow in the brush and thick bushes, he had his hand over my mouth as we knelt on the ground. He'd carried me here.

"Don't make a sound. Stay down," he whispered. I nodded but he must have seen my indecision in my eyes as he took his hand away. "CB, I am the most serious I have ever been in my entire life," he said, his words rough. "You stay here and wait for me, no matter what you hear or see, you got me?" I tried to nod but it apparently wasn't good enough. He jerked my chin up so I had to look directly into his face. "Answer me," he commanded.

"What's going on?"

"Trouble, that's what. They will not hesitate to…hurt you, Clara. Answer me," he almost growled.

"Ok," I whispered in response.

He kissed me roughly and then put his thumb over my lips. His violet eyes begged me to obey him. "I can't lose you," he mouthed, but I still heard. "Please."

I understood. I couldn't lose him either, not now. I nodded. "I promise," I replied as strong as I could.

"I'm immortal. They can't hurt me," he assured quietly. "They only way they can get to me is through you. Say it."

"I understand, I'll stay."

"I have no idea what's going to happen but you must not come out for any reason. We have to do this the right way, and them meeting you here like this is not."

"Ok."

"I…" He gulped. "You're all I have."

"I won't move a muscle, I won't come out, I'll be quiet, I promise. Besides, I'm not the hero type."

He chuckled uneasily and chided me, "Clara, not the time."

"Be careful," I said, my voice grating and cracking.

"One more thing," he edged and it seemed like he didn't want to say it. "They'll see the string so you have to hide it. Only you can hide it," he continued when I opened my mouth to argue. "It might be uncomfortable, but it's the only way. You have to pull it back in your mind and hold it. It'll push against you, it'll want to get back to me but you have to hold on tight."

I nodded, what else could I do, and said, "Show me what to do."

He told me to mentally pull it in my mind, like I was using my fingers to yank it toward me. I did that and felt it tugging back. It was true, it didn't want to leave Eli. I felt angry for no apparent reason. Eli pulled my face up.

"It's ok. I know it sucks, just do it. Hurry."

I did it again and saw it detaching itself from his wrist. Eli's face grimaced and he groaned. At first I thought it was because he was picking up my emotion but no…his skin bloomed a blue spot that grew the more I pulled. His blood. I looked horrified up to him.

"Hold it," he hissed. "Don't let go or we'll have to do it again."

I kept my mental hold on the string and watched as it pulled and raced from his wrist up his arm, like pulling a cord from a wall, all the way to his chest. I felt it yank all of a sudden and enter my wrist and a zing shot up my arm to my chest. Eli fell back from the force of it and grunted. The pressure of it, pushing and pressing against my ribs, was uncomfortable as he had said, but it was more than that. It felt wrong. I looked back to his shirt.

"Is that your blood? Why are you bleeding?" I asked him as he sat back up. "Your chest…your arm…"

"Well…" he groaned a little as he took off his now destroyed white shirt and pulled back on his black button up, rolling down the sleeves, "it was attached." As he buttoned the sleeve I saw the angry black skin around the hole as it still oozed blue.

"Then why did we do it?" I said angrily. "I wouldn't have done that to you had you told me-"

"And that is why," he interrupted, "I didn't tell you. I knew you would never have been able to hurt me but we needed it done so they won't follow the string back to you."

I held back my tears at his sacrifice. He was trying to keep me safe, apparently at all cost. Instead, I told him him a half truth.

"I'm going to be mad at you about this later," I told him quietly and too softly for the threat to be credible.

He nodded and kissed me again, but this time it wasn't rough. In fact, it was creamy and fluid as he pressed his lips to mine. I gripped his arm to convey the thought that I didn't want him to go. He lingered in my space for a second before moving away and shooting through the woods behind us. When I looked for him in the park I saw him emerge from the other side. He was trying to divert someone from my location. But who?

"Mr. Thames," a gruff male accented voice called, "I'm delighted to have you join us."

"Everyone here knows that's not true, Hatch. Let's get right down to the matter, if you don't mind." I saw Angelina come up near Eli but he gave her a look that said to keep her distance. Surprisingly, she did. I still couldn't see anyone else in the field as Eli went on. "Angelina called you unnecessarily. We don't have a problem here."

"Really? My dear Angelina, tell a lie?" Hatch laughed gravelly. "If we're playing the honest card, I assumed that she was spouting lies since it was concerning you. I knew she was just trying to end whatever it was that you started in this town."

"And yet you came," Eli muttered quietly. "Why?"

"Because they have to," Angelina interrupted smartly and grinned. "What would our people say if the Horde plays pick and choose instead of following credible leads?"

"Bite your tongue, wench," one of Hatch's men growled.

"Whoa, Miles. We'll have our turn with her," Hatch said and looked back to her face that had suddenly gone white, "in the mean time, we need to determine what's going on here. Eli, care to elaborate?"

"I mated with a human here and Angelina can't handle rejection."

Everyone laughed and it echoed and bounced around me. It sounded like there were lots of them out there. Then one of them stepped forward and the trees were no longer in my line of sight. I assumed it was Hatch. He was a large man with cannonballs in the arms of his jacket. Or I guess it was just his arms. I tried to tamp down on my fright so they wouldn't feel me there.

He crossed his arms and cocked his head looking at the ground. Enoch's prone form still lay there and he kicked Enoch's head with his boot to make it roll to the other side. I felt bile rise but held it together. The pressure in my chest was almost painful now.

"And poor, Enoch," he laughed and nudged him once more in the shoulder for good measure. "Not playing nice was he?"

"He was trying to save a feeler girl from me," Angelina explained. "Eli is the one telling lies. A human bonded herself to him," she shrieked.

Everyone stilled. I knew that was it, the thing that Eli had been so afraid of. Mating was ok, it even seemed to be well looked upon, but for some reason bonding was not. I watched in frightful anticipation as Hatch's men gathered closer around them.

"Where is my connection then?" Eli held his arms wide. "Where is she?"

"She was here earlier," Angelina insisted frantically. "I saw the string myself!"

"I took her home to sleep," Eli said as if bored. "Can't have my plaything getting too tired to play, now can I?"

Hatch laughed and looked Eli over closely. "I heard you were in the capitol."

"I was," Eli replied, "but country bumpkins suit me."

Another round of laughter that had Angelina's veins becoming bold in her arms and wrists. "He had her here and they are bloody bonded! I saw it with my own eyes!"

"Eli's right. If they were bonded, there would be a string," Hatch said smoothly.

"But you can pull back the string," she rebutted. "You can hide it."

"From what I hear it's agonizing. Are you in agony, Eli?" Hatch asked slyly.

"Yes, but not from a bond. From red heads with too much time on their hands."

Hatch came forward then and clapped Eli on the shoulder before saying, "Besides, I think Eli is too smart to let something so stupid happen to him.

Keeping our mate unhappily satisfied is the whole point, right? Gratitude in painful pleasure and all that?"

Eli stayed silent. Angelina puffed her ragged breaths into the air between them. I was so focused on the string I barely felt the cold. It pressed harder every time I thought about it. I felt a thud against my chest that resounded down my arm and realized I was about to be losing my battle with it. It wanted Eli as much as I did.

"Me, of course," Hatch continued and made his way around Eli to Angelina's side, "I prefer a different treat every night. I'm not the mating type, but to each his own."

"Until it comes to bonding," Angelina spouted.

"Yes," he drawled, "until it comes to bonding. I'm doing our race a favor by getting rid of the traitors who threaten to pollute our young with human blood."

Pollute with human blood? Devourers and humans could have children? The string yanked in my chest and I actually fell forward to the ground with the force. Luckily, I landed in dirt, not crunchy leaves, and my fall was silent. I glanced back up and held a hand to my chest as if that would help.

Eli visibly looked shaken for a second. He gripped his chest and grit his teeth prompting Hatch to ask, "Something wrong?"

"No. I'm just ready to be done with this," he answered steadily.

"As am I. Angelina, I see no cause for your summons of the Horde. We are busy people, what with dealing with humans who find out about us, the few and far between traitors, the ones who wish to change our ways. I resent this waste of my time."

"But, Hatch," she yelled and stepped forward a little, "they are bonded. They're…hiding it somehow."

"I see no evidence to that and I don't take lives lightly. If he was bonded with a feeler and can hide is this well, then kudos to him." He moved forward and trailed a finger down her arm. "As for you however, I say we have more to discuss. Bring her," he snapped to someone and she was snatched into big arms. They carried her off as she screamed and bucked against them, but they held steady. Hatch started to follow them but stopped. "I'd leave this town, Elijah. It's never good to stay in one place for too long."

"I've been thinking that myself," Eli answered easily and crossed his arms. "See you around, Hatch."

"Yeah…around."

And then he, too, moved towards his men at a pace that was swift and too quick to be normal. As soon as they were gone, I waited. I knew Eli was making sure they were gone. I counted the seconds…1…2…3...4…5…6…7. The bond jerked, and this time I couldn't contain my grunt. It hurt. I looked up to Eli at the exact second that his resolve ended…or maybe it was mine.

He came careening toward me through the air; upright, but his feet were dragging the ground. He tried to stop, slow down, something, but even as he swatted limbs away from him, he plowed into me and we toppled to the ground. The bond wound itself around his wrist and I felt almost as if my insides sighed.

"Oh, Clara, I'm sorry. I couldn't stop," he pleaded and raked my hair back from my face. "Are you all right?"

"I am now," I answered truthfully.

"I am so sorry," he said vehemently and kissed my forehead. "I hate that you had to go through that, but it was the only way to keep you safe."

"It's ok. I see now. That Hatch guy isn't a fan."

"No," he agreed and once again his hand moved across my face and neck, my arm, my stomach and side. "You're all right? Did it hurt?"

"Not at first, but the longer we held out the worst it was."

"That was incredible," he told me, the awe evident in his voice. "The stories of this kind of thing are skewed and fairy taled, but I've never heard of a bond being held back that long."

"Well, I'm not a normal human. Or should I say feeler."

"Don't say that word," he said. "I've always hated it and I wanted to punch every person out there that said it about you."

I touched his cheek, my middle finger rubbing across his eyebrow ring. He closed his eyes and exhaled. I felt his whole body relax from its tense position. I felt his weight on me as he let me help to relax him. The ground beneath was surprisingly comfortable, though cold, and I continued to reassure him with my touch for a few more moments before he lifted his head once more.

"I'm so glad you're ok," he said, but the words barely made a sound. "I was aching with worry for you, thinking the bond was hurting you. I thought that was better than death, though."

"It's ok now. It's over," I assured, but thought. "Isn't it?"

"I'm afraid to think so." His nose was almost touching mine as he gazed down at me. "I'll keep watch outside your house tonight, just to be sure." He let his thumb run the length of my eyebrow and then down my cheek. "Clara, we have a lot of things to talk about."

"Like what?"

"Like whether it's safe to stay here now."

"I can't leave at the end of Senior year," I said.

"Will it even matter if you're not alive to enjoy it?" he countered.

"Ok, point taken. But for the record, I want to stay here until then."

"We'll talk about it later."

I nodded and rubbed his shirt front, but didn't let my fingers press into his skin just in case. I let my fingers almost skim the length of his arm to his wrist.

"How's this doing?"

"All better," he said low and rumbling. "I just needed you."

I pulled him down by his collar and kissed him gratefully. He was alive, I was alive, we'd made it through whoever those guys were, his evil twin, me binding myself to him and his crazy stalker semi-ex. It had been quite a night. I felt his knees lift until he was kneeling over me, but he didn't leave me. He put an arm under my back and lifted me to be closer to him.

His warmth and the warmth my body was creating on its own from being completely affected by him was enough to make me comfortable again. He eased away gently and sighed against my skin. Then he kissed my forehead and put a hand out to steady himself, but he jerked back with a hiss.

"What?" I asked.

"Thorns."

I took his hand and looked at it. A thorn had pricked his thumb, barely, big baby. I smiled and without even thinking, put it in my mouth to make it feel better. What in the world made me do that? He watched me, enthralled by my actions, and sucked in a breath as I ran my tongue along his skin. I released him and then kissed it. He looked at it and then back to me. The look on his face was hard to decipher. Was he grossed out? Was he perplexed by my human behavior and need to comfort?

"Stop," he whispered. "I don't ever want to feel your insecurity around me again." He pushed me back down to the ground and followed me on his knees like before. "I'm fascinated by you, that's all. You're unlike any human I've ever come across before. The things you say and do…the way you react to things… It's all I can do to keep up with you. I think you are going to be very entertaining in the days to come."

"Hey," I muttered.

He smiled that smirk that made me first wonder how I was ever going to resist him. And now I didn't have to. He pulled me up again, just like before, and his mouth found mine easily. He held me so effortlessly and didn't need my help, but I gripped his arms anyway just to feel him real and there under my fingertips.

We heard a grunt and froze, his lips still on mine. We waited for another noise, another clue. Then we heard it again and Eli put a finger to my lips to remind me to stay quiet. I nodded as he raised himself up to stand. Then he rolled his eyes and sighed before pulling me up with him.

"My idiotic brother is awake. We better scram before he remembers what happened and takes it out on us," he said, but he laughed as he pulled me along, easing my fears.

Fifteen

Eli took me to his house first. Luckily, somehow, it wasn't time for my curfew yet.

He said he wanted to clean both of us up before taking me home.

He opened the door and I took a good look around as he ushered me in. It looked the same as before, plain and old fashioned. He took my hand and pulled me through the house, right passed that bird. I swear its eyes followed us across the room.

"What's up with the bird?"

"I told you, it's a nasty vile creature. I hate that bird," he explained as he opened a door to a long line down of dark stairs. "My room."

"So," I asked as I braved the stairs ahead of him, "if you hate the bird so much, why do you keep it?"

"It's immortal," he sneered as if that idea upset him.

"What?" I asked and turned on the stairs to look at him. He grabbed a pull string above his head and the area around us illuminated. You'd think a basement would be dank and dusty, but it looked just like any other room, although huge. The walls were black stucco and the floor was white tile. It was so clean I was afraid to walk on it. A huge wooden post bed sat in the middle of the room against the wall. The room was freakishly sterile and organized, as if no one lived there at all. The bed was smooth and clean like a hotel bed-make job. I looked at him and quirked a brow.

"What?" he asked smoothly as his eyes followed me from his perch on the back wall.

"Anal much?"

He laughed that delicious deep chuckle that gave me goose bumps just hearing it...letting alone feeling it rumble as he was suddenly at my back.

"I have to say, I like you in my room."

I turned to him slowly and peeked up at him, fully expecting a Tate face; open mouth, droopy passion induced eyes and a tight neck from strain because he could never seem to control himself. I wondered if I should regret coming down to his room. Would he think it was an invitation? But as my eyes found his, I saw that he was himself. His lips held a smile, but it wasn't cocky or flirty. It was sweet. He really just liked the idea of me in his space. And given by the apparent lack of guests, I couldn't say I blamed him.

"Me, too," I answered and smiled back. "Are you going to keep staying here?"

"I don't see why not."

"Um, maybe because the Horde and your evil-ex know where you live?" I spouted sarcastically and fisted my hands to my hips.

"She is *not* my ex," he said smartly.

"Whatever, you know what I mean."

"Uhuh, I do. That you are particularly intriguing when you're jealous."

"Well, it's a little disconcerting…the whole a-goddess-wants-my-boyfriend thing."

He laughed again and hooked his fingers in my front pockets to pull me to him.

"You are one cute human." He tipped my chin with a crooked finger. "Did you not see the whole me-choosing-you-over-her thing," he said mockingly.

I tried to scowl, tried to frown, bit my lip to stop the smile, but it won, hands down.

"Yeah, that was pretty sweet," I agreed.

"Yeah. Now, let's get you a clean shirt and get you home before I have to add 'Pastor' to my list of growing enemies."

"Why does the Horde care if we're together?" I asked as I took my shirt off when his back was turned to rummage through his dresser drawers. I held my shirt over my front. He turned and stumbled a little at seeing me that way, but held the shirt out as he turned back around.

I accepted the t-shirt he gave me and hoped that no one noticed my shirt was different at home.

"Well," he cleared his throat, "what he said about polluting our race, he believes that. The Horde does. They are a group who takes matters into their own hands and places those of us that they deem a traitor into custody. And they kill humans who interfere with our kind or find out about us."

"So, they're like your council or police or something?" I asked as I pulled the shirt over my head and smoothed the front. Teenage Mutant Ninja Turtles. I smirked as he went on.

"No, not at all. We have no government, no council, no regulations, no laws. That would defeat the whole purpose in their eyes, though the hypocrisy is almost funny." He turned his profile towards me. "Can I turn around now?"

"Yes, I'm decent. As decent as I *can* be wearing super hero turtles from the 90's."

He looked me over and smiled wistfully as he said, "I love that shirt."

"I'll make sure you get it back."

"No problem. You'll be with me anyway won't you? I'll just take it back if I want it." He pulled me by my hands and sat me on the bed. "Now, see, they think mating is acceptable because, as I said, it's all about control. They've never accepted nor understood a bonding and I've never personally met anyone who has been. But I knew it would be trouble, I just assumed we'd lay low and then avoid my kind at all cost. But Enoch and Angelina couldn't make things easy for us, could they?" he spat angrily and clenched his fists on the bed between us. I covered my hand with his, smoothing the angry blue veins.

I waited for him to say something. I didn't try to soothe him with empty words.

He continued, "We're going to have to do a lot of pretending. A lot of...lying. A lot of trying to avoid my kind."

"Are they going to be coming after us or something?"

"I don't know if the Horde bought it or not. They're very manipulative and sneaky. They may have just been playing us, but they took Angelina so...I don't know. I just know that I can't leave you alone. Not yet."

"Eli," I countered, "you can't just sit outside my house every night, all night."

"Of course I can, CB," he replied almost smugly. "You can't stop me, so don't even try. I know I can't come in, but I can at least watch out for you while you sleep."

"But you'll be…bored. You'll get tired of me pretty quick that way," I grumbled.

He scooted closer and put a hand around the front of my neck, using his thumb to tip up my chin as he said, "Have I not made my feelings for you clear?"

"Yes, but-"

"Nothing. Absolutely nothing is more important than you. Besides," he pulled me closer and put an arm around my shoulder, "I like the night. It's quiet. It's easy to deal with. I've lived a very fast paced and reckless life and to be able to just sit and enjoy peace is a gift all its own. And sitting outside your window, knowing you're safe inside, is just icing."

"Ok," I conceded, "if you must. But I don't want you putting yourself in danger either."

He nodded and chuckled a little. "Ok, CB. You got it."

"So tell me about the bird. It's immortal?" I asked, continuing my earlier question.

He shifted uncomfortably, pulling his arm from me and leaning his elbows on his knees. He fingered the barbed string on his wrist and avoided my gaze. I thought, that couldn't be good. I leaned forward, too, and asked him the silent question with my eyes. He sighed and finally looked up to see me. "It's Angelina's bird."

"What?" I asked and sat up.

"It's Ange-"

"I heard you!" I almost yelled and he looked away again. I felt suddenly hysterical. Why would he have her bird if nothing went on and why wouldn't he have told me about it? "Why do you have her bird?" I tried for calm.

"She abandoned it on one of her escapades to come and get me. She's had that blasted bird for as long as I can remember. I've always hated it. She taught it to say all kinds of stupid things." He looked back to me. "I know you think it proves me guilty of lying to you, but I haven't. She left it, I don't know why, but she did and I couldn't just leave it there, too. Number one, it's immortal as I said and number two, as badly as I don't like the thing, it's an animal. It doesn't have to eat to survive, but it feels hunger and it was cruel to leave it there in that cave in California for all eternity, hungry and alone. Besides if a human had found it there's no telling what they would've done with it."

I stared at him in awe. Really? That's why he wanted to hide all that? Because he thought I would assume he was lying?

"Eli-"

"I didn't want you to think I had feelings for her still or that I was keeping the bird as some love trinket or reminder."

"I wouldn't-"

"In all honesty, it just makes me soft to keep it, but I couldn't help it. I've had the bird for 21 years now and believe me, I have no love for that bird. It hasn't spoken a word to me. I'm not sure what that's about, but..." He looked back to me and his eyes pleaded with me. "Please forgive me. I meant to tell you, but it just snowballed and then my omission felt like a lie and then you met her and it seemed like it was too late to say anything then; that the evidence was too damning."

"Eli, you're nuts," I said when I could finally get a word in.

"What?" he asked, completely confused.

"You really think that after everything that you said today and everything that happened to us at the park with Angelina that I would think you still have feelings for her?"

He smirked a ghost of a smile. "Well…I just didn't want to hurt you."

"I don't care who the bird belongs to. It's really sweet that you saved it, especially since you find it so revolting."

He laughed. "Really? I thought you were going to throw some human hissy fit over this."

"Well, it sucks that you didn't tell me and it sucks even worse that you think I'd leave you over it or something, but I don't care. It's just a bird."

"It's not just a bird," he told me and took my hand to run this thumb over my wrist over and over. "He's immortal. You didn't think to ask me about it?"

"Honestly, Eli, I'm not sure I can even be surprised anymore at this point," I answered and was caught off guard by how breathless I sounded.

I watched him continue to torture my wrist with his slow fluid skimming movements. He seemed completely engrossed in what he was doing. When I could take it now longer and goose bumps spread rapidly up my arm, that seemed to snap him back to the present. He turned his gaze to mine and smiled, in satisfaction as much as happiness.

He continued to smile as he spoke. "The bird has a spell on it. When Angelina got it in the 1700's, she was dealing a lot with witches and sorcerers back then."

"Witches and sorcerers?" I squeaked. "What do you mean?"

"I mean that I'm not the only nightmare out there."

"There are other things," I mused and nodded, breathing through bits and spurts of panic. "Like what?"

"Well," he said slowly and pulled my hand to cradle it against his chest, "I'm not going to tell you. I want your dreams to be only good things. Well, and me, of course."

"Eli," I snapped, half because I was scared and half because I didn't want him to spend the rest of our lives acting like we were opposite sides of the good-vs.-evil spectrum, "stop acting like you're evil."

"I am evil," he insisted with a slight tightening of his jaw. "And no matter how tame you think I am, you'd do well to remember that."

"Why?"

"So when I do wind up doing something in the future that you may not approve of, you won't be so shocked about it."

"Like what you did to that security guard at the club that night?" I asked softly.

He looked at me sharply before saying, "You noticed that?"

I nodded. "What did you do?"

"I just persuaded him to let you in."

"How?"

"I'm not without my talents," he growled in what sounded like frustration before combing his hands through his hair and leaning on his elbows to his knees once more. "I'm sorry. I immediately regretted it once I did it, but it was the only way to get you in. And I didn't know you understood what I'd done for what it was."

"You didn't hurt him," I said and thought back to that night. "He wasn't scared, you just persuaded him."

"Exactly. Persuading - making people think they want what we want - is another one of our tricks," he muttered. "It's so addictive and easy because it's subtle. It's so very easy to just plant a seed of what we want in their mind. I hadn't done it in a long time, but that night I just…I wanted to spend time with you and it just happened," he admitted and the shame of his words practically coated the air.

"Eli," I turned his face to look at me, "I'll help you. Do you understand?" He shook his head and scrunched his eyebrows. I knelt on the floor in between his knees and put my hands on his legs. "Ok, listen. Once, a long time ago, in my parent's marriage, my dad was having a hard time at work. We went through a rough patch and almost lost our house. He started drinking. For about a month, my dad was drunk almost every minute of every day when he was laid off from his job. Well, my mom let him try to work through everything, but eventually, she had to step in. She went on a rampage, going through the whole house and throwing away every bottle she could find, his cigarettes, everything. He followed her around and yelled at her as she did it, but he never touched her, never forced her to stop. Do you know why?"

He shook his head a 'no'.

"Because he loved her. Because deep down, he wanted her to do it. He needed her help. He wasn't strong enough to drop the shoe himself, but he was willing to let her do it for him. He trusted her and needed her and she knew it. It was the only time in their marriage where they had problems, and after that, they were practically inseparable. It was kind of gross actually," I said remembering and smiled. "But my point is that I get it. You're the protective type, you're the big, bad Devourer." He cracked his first smile and I felt my held breath release and relax in gratitude for it. "But even though I might need you to save me, a lot, I'll always be here for *you*. I'd never let you lose yourself or go back to something you were before. I can save you if I have to and I'll fight with everything I have." I pointed to our wrists where the string held tight. "I think I've proven that already."

His breaths were loud and laced with strain. I didn't know why, I thought he'd understand what I was trying to say. Then he pulled me up by my elbows, wrapping his arms around me completely and pressed his mouth to mine. He sighed a long and needed breath that seemed to relax even the tension in the air. I put my arms around his neck, for my own need to be held up as anything else. He was answering me, letting me know that he was grateful. And boy, was he being thorough. His hands pressed me and slid over me in caresses that were meant to show affection and devotion. That was all.

Once again, I felt safe in every way possible and it made me ache in my chest with gratitude.

It seemed like this was something he needed more than wanted to do, like he was being pulled to it without a will in it, so I let him ravish and devour me for quite a while before he finally pulled back, but not by much.

With his hand on my cheek and his rough breaths against my neck, he looked down at me almost as if embarrassed by his actions.

"Sorry," he said, confirming my thoughts.

"Why would you be sorry for that?" I whispered and licked my lip to feel it plump and tender from his kisses.

"I just...I needed to feel the way you feel about me," he admitted. "Nothing makes me feel more human, more capable of being good, more like I could possibly deserve something like this one day, than when I kiss you...and you kiss me back, completely of your own free will."

I sighed. "I need you to stop being so self deprecating," I said, going for firm and stern, but my mind was still reeling from what he said. He laughed and shook his head. "Eli," I sighed his name, thinking of a way to make him see, "what you said was so…I've always wanted someone to feel that way about me. I feel the same way about you. I mean, without the human part," he laughed again as I kept going, "but I was always a prize; a toy to be paraded around. When I'm with you, I feel like I know what my parents had was real. They loved each other, no matter what, no matter what demons came into their lives. I'd almost given up that that was possible anymore."

"It's not impossible, CB," he said softly, sweeping a hand down my arm to twine his fingers with mine. "You're the best intrusion that has ever invaded my life. I'll be forever grateful that I found you."

I never thought being called an intrusion would make me cry, but I was about to. I nodded to him, as it was all I could do, and he kissed my fingers. This was so much, so fast, but, gosh, did I need it. Despite what he said about his needing me, I needed him.

"Now," he edged, sensing I wanted a subject change to stave off red, crying eyes all night, "you have more questions for me, right?"

"Yes." I cleared my throat. "Ok, about the bird," he grunted in annoyance, "you say he's immortal. Did Angelina buy him that way or did she have him cursed after she bought him."

"We'll never know. She's not very forthcoming."

"But you say you found the bird in a cave in California?"

"It was my cave," he said carefully and never removed his eyes from mine.

"Your cave," I repeated. "Then how did the bird get there?"

He sighed and squeezed my fingers a bit, stalling. I quirked a brow at him. He ventured on.

"Angelina brought the bird with her everywhere. She and Enoch were really relentless in their efforts to find me. Sometimes, it was worth it to exchange amenities for comfort, if it meant that I could not see them for longer."

"Ah. So you stayed in caves and places where they wouldn't think to look for you," I realized.

"Yes. But they always found me eventually."

"So…"I said, finally getting what he was saying. "Angelina was in the cave with you."

Sixteen

"Yeah," he answered gruffly and looked up to me. "She left the bird there once when she went to come after me. I went back to the cave after some time and saw that she had abandoned it. She's never tried to take it back since." He took a deep breath. "I'll be honest, you deserve that. I never brought it up before because there was never a reason to, but she would find me and I would pretend with her sometimes."

"Pretend what?" I asked and it came out shrill. I cleared my throat.

"Pretend to be what she wanted," he confessed. I tensed and his arms around me tightened a bit to keep me there.

"But you told me you were never with her," I accused.

"I wasn't. Never. I would never lie to you. She'd show up and there was no way to leave unless I bolted and she'd be too close behind. I had to distract her so I could catch her off guard and get a head start. So, sometimes…I would act like I was surrendering. I'd let her kiss me. She was so gullible, she believed that I had caved. She'd let her guard down and when she ran errands or went to feed, I'd run, leaving everything behind."

"No wonder she follows you, Eli," I chastised softly, "after you led her on like that."

"I didn't lead her on. I tried to just leave, I tried to tell her the truth - that there was absolutely no future for us - but she never gave in. I was losing my mind. Can you imagine running from someone for hundreds of years as they chased you and ruined your life over and over again?" He huffed a surprised breath. "I can't believe you're taking her side anyway."

"I'm not taking her side. I just know how girls think."

"Not this girl," he assured me. "We're talking about 'Psycho' meets 'The Babysitter'," he explained, making me snicker. He pulled my face up to look at him closely. "You don't ever have to worry about her and me. There's no history there, just bad memories."

"I'm not worried."

"Anyway, it's not like you had to see it for yourself. Unlike me, I saw you and Tate everywhere and in large quantities if you recall; at lunch, at diners, at your locker, at your house," he said wryly.

"Ok, I get it. I have no room to talk." That sure gave me some perspective. "I was just trying to…with Tate I just…"

"I know what you were *just* doing. You were just trying to stop your feelings for me by making out with your boyfriend who you weren't in love with."

"Yes, that's what I was doing," I admitted. "I felt guilty for feeling anything for you when I still had a boyfriend."

He pulled me closer and whispered into my hair, "And it made me respect you even more for it. Let's just forget about that. I think it all worked out for the best, don't you?"

"Yeah." I leaned back. "I better get going."

"I'll walk you," he said and I knew better than to argue.

As we made our way upstairs and passed the living room I stopped at the birds' cage. He looked at me with a crooked neck. He blinked, I blinked.

"Cavuto," I said and it stayed silent. "Cavuto want a cracker?" Still nothing.

I rolled my eyes and went to leave, hearing Eli chuckle behind me, but we both stopped when we heard from behind us, "Arequipa."

"Arawhata?" I asked as we both turned back to the bird.

"Arequipa," Eli repeated. "It's a city in Peru. Angelina must have taken the bird there at some point."

"Have you ever been there?"

"Yeah…about 25 years ago. It's been a while. But I wasn't there with her," he finished quickly.

"OK, well, let's-"

"Clara want a cracker?"

"What?" I asked and laughed nervously as I glanced at Eli. He looked stunned, too. "That bird is pretty chatty. I thought you said he never talked?"

"Yeah." He crossed his arms in contemplation. "I haven't heard him speak since I took him. He must like you. Maybe he just likes girls."

I went closer to the cage and crooned to him, "How did you know my name, little guy?"

"Eli told me, idiot."

I stilled and glared at the bird. The innocent little feathery beast was perched on his feet from his swing so sweetly, like he didn't just insult me. I switched my gaze to Eli, who was smothering a laugh in his fist. Very badly, I might add.

"Ah, CB," he soothed. "I told you she taught it to be foul mouthed."

"Ok, fine. Bye, Cavuto, you deviant little thing."

"Bye, toots," the bird sang out.

Before I could turn and teach that bird a few new choice words, Eli had grabbed me and turned us out the door. He was still fighting a smile as we walked to my house.

"Not funny," I muttered. "I can't even get birds to show me some respect."

He pulled me under his arm and said, "I respect you."

"Yeah, but you're only one person. Everyone else thinks I'm a ditz or a tease or, recently, a stupid human."

"You are none of those things." He kissed my temple as we turned into my yard. "I told you, the bird has said way nastier things in the time that I've known him."

"So," I thought of some more of the questions I wanted to ask before he was gone. "The Sweet Grass carnival is coming up."

"And the dance."

"Yeah, but I'm not going to that."

"Why? You don't think I'd want to go?"

"I don't want to."

"There's got to be a reason," he asked softly as we reached my porch and turned to face each other.

"The old me would have loved to have gone. The new me, not so much. The carnival, yes, I'm dying to go. But the dance is just a juvenile and pointless thing that I don't need nor want to do when there are plenty of other things to round out my education. For the first time in my life, I feel like I'm in control of myself." I smiled up at him.

"Well, I'm glad then." His hands coasted up and down my arms. "But I am going to wish I could've seen you in a pretty, silky dress."

"Well," I thought, "there's always prom."

"So we're not ditching all school functions, just the ones you dub as juvenile?"

"Now you're getting it," I jested and poked his stomach. He laughed as he pulled me to him.

"I'll be here all night," he promised. "You'll be safe, so I want you to sleep tight."

"You won't put yourself in danger will you?"

"Nah, I'll be fine."

"I'm not particularly thrilled about you being out here alone."

"My whole life, I've been alone."

"That's doesn't make it ok for now."

"Clara, don't argue. When it comes to you being safe, I won't ever compromise on that." I scowled up at him. "And don't pout. It doesn't work on me. I'm immune," he said grinning.

"I highly doubt that," I said in a challenging tone.

He just smiled that crooked, gorgeous smile that fit his lips perfectly and kissed me. "I'm not going to come to you in a Reverie tonight. You need your rest. Enoch will be too exhausted from recuperating to try and Angelina, hopefully, is indisposed."

"Ok," I said reluctantly. I liked the Reveries. We could go wherever we wanted for any kind of weather. It was our own little fantasy world. "If you change your mind though, I'll be all for it," I told him and pulled him down to me once more.

He chuckled huskily against my lips. When we parted this time he looked down at our wrists. He rubbed mine and smiled without looking up. "Thank you for this."

"You're welcome. Thank you for picking me first."

"Always will," he said with promise. Then he rubbed my cheek and turned to go, calling over his shoulder, "I'll be here all night. Stay inside and sleep well."

"Ok. Thank you," was all I could say. He wasn't exactly giving me much choice.

I turned to go inside and ran down the hall in the quiet house. I glanced in the mirror before taking off Eli's shirt and did a double take. My eyes were seriously green, like Eli had said. I liked the way it made me look; different in a familiar way that made me feel mysterious and empowered. Wow. How to explain this one…

I showered quickly and went to lay on my bed in an exhausted heap. I flopped on my back, my arms spread wide and I looked at my wrist. The barb wire was still wrapped around me in its possession and made a path out my window to wherever Eli was. I felt satisfied with just that small reminder that I belonged to him. And vice versa.

I smiled as I rolled over and closed my eyes. And though I was by myself in the dark of my room and the dark of my eyelids, I knew Eli was right there outside and I've never in my life felt so looked after and safe.

~ ~ ~

The next morning, I woke a little early. It was pretty quiet in the house so I hurried and got ready for the day. With my uniform on and hair fixed, I ran downstairs to fix a glass of juice. Pastor snuck, unintentionally, up on me and made me spill some of the orange juice on the counter.

"Sorry. Thought you heard me."

"It's ok. Just a little jumpy, I guess," I answered as I sopped juice into a paper towel.

"So, what's on the…" he started, but trailed off as his newspaper fell to the counter and he came closer. "What happened to your eyes?"

"Oh," I laughed nervously and rehearsed the explanation I'd concocted this morning, "it's a social experiment for school. You know, to see how many people look you in the eye when they talk to you. I'm going to see how many notice my eye color is different."

"Interesting. I like it. And the green actually suits you well, it was just a shock."

"No worries. Bye!"

"Bye."

I was glad he didn't ask me why I was leaving so early. I had to see Eli before school and since he was nowhere to be found in my yard, and the string had me heading into the woods, I headed for his house to wait for him instead. When I got there I knocked softly, but remembered he wasn't there yet and rolled my eyes at myself before I went inside. The bird was asleep with a sheet over the top so I crept by, happy to escape anymore interactions with the rude thing.

I made my way down the stairs to his room and found something I had not intended. Instead of an empty room that I could sit and wait for Eli in, I found Angelina. And she was awake, naked, covered only in his black silk sheets, in his bed.

Seventeen

She roused slowly and languidly, stretching and pretending like she couldn't see me there. The sheet fell away from her chest to her waist and I couldn't help the disgusted gasp that fell from my lips. Or the following ,"Oh, please."

"Yeah, right," she muttered and finally looked my way. "Don't act like you're not impressed."

"Are you serious?" I said incredulously and shielded my eyes. "Viewer discretion is advised."

"I know what I look like to my own kind, let alone human standards," she said matter-of-factly and suavely pushed and smoothed her hair back before pulling the sheet back up.

"You are a real piece of work," I said sharply and crossed my arms over my uniformed chest. I felt silly in my uniform in this setting, with her laying there so perfectly. "Who do you think you are?"

"I'm who Eli was with last night," she replied happily and smiled, a cruel grin on her pink lips. "And I gotta tell you, coming back together after all that chasing was so worth it."

It hit me like a message from the sky; a plan.

I dropped my chin to my chest, to stop the grin more than anything else, because I wanted her to believe that I believed her. I turned to go, slowly, carefully. I heard her giggle behind me and turned, where she could just see my profile.

"I hope you're happy," I said softly.

"Oh, I am," she affirmed. "Couldn't be happier."

I left walking straight back to my house. I wasn't exactly sure where my plan started and ended, but I knew that they had to think that Eli was leaving me. If I started the bond then couldn't I stop it somehow? Not that I wanted to, but if he left, then they'd stop coming after us right? He could come back for me later.

They had to believe it though; the Horde, Enoch, Angelina, everyone.

I came back into my yard just as Eli and Enoch were coming around the back. Enoch looked all too smug and it clicked into place for me. Him and Angelina planned this whole thing. He had come and gotten Eli, knowing I'd go looking for him when I got up, and Angelina set herself up at Eli's house.

Bastard and witch! It wasn't too hard to portray feelings of anger for Enoch to feel because I was pissed.

"Where have you been?" Eli growled as he came to me. "I was just about to follow the string to you. I thought we talked about this? You can't just wander around by yourself!"

"Oh, like you care," I said and even though it wasn't real for me, it hurt so much to see the rejection on his face when I said, "Like you were really waiting here all night for me."

"What? What are you talking about?"

"I know about Angelina! I went to your house, I saw her in your bed. I know everything."

"Clara, you have to see this for what it is. I was not with Angelina, I was here, all night, like I promised you. They're trying to trick you."

"The evidence speaks for itself, I think. I'm so done here," I said and pushed between them to go to my back door. Eli grabbed my arm and when I turned, it was almost too much. His face was twisted in horror and disbelief. He begged me silently to hear him out, that he could explain everything, but I couldn't. If we were going to trick Enoch and Angelina into thinking that they had tricked us first, then I had to go inside away from him. Now.

"Let go," I said and when he continued to stare, I yelled it, "Let go!"

He did immediately and watched me go inside my house. I leaned on the door with my back and slid down. I knew I was going to be late to school now, but I didn't care much about that. I needed to get Eli to follow me into a Reverie so he knew what I was doing.

I closed my eyes, tight. I waited. He didn't come. I figured he needed time to get rid of Enoch, first. I waited some more but he still didn't come. I almost stood to go and find him, to tell him it was all just a hoax on them but we needed them to believe it. We needed them to leave town.

The next time I glanced at the clock, it had been twenty minutes. I could take it no longer. I ran back outside but they were gone already. I searched everywhere, even called his name a few times, risking to blow my plan, but never heard a sound. I ran into the street and followed the string with my eyes but it just went on and on.

I ran back inside to my room, closed the door and sat on my bed. I begged him in my mind, forced my thoughts to be his. I threw myself back onto the bed and felt a hot angry tear as it slid from my eye down into my hairline. I said things in my mind to him, begging him to come to me as I squeezed my eyes shut so tight it hurt.

"Clara?" I heard and jerked up to see Eli in my room. I jumped up and threw my arms around him. "Clara, I thought you…"

"That I what?" I asked and leaned back. "That I hated you? I'm not sure that's possible."

"But you…I mean you were so… And how did you pull me into a Reverie?"

"I did this?"

He nodded as he said, "I was burning sheets one second and the next, I was here watching you on your bed."

"Burning sheets?"

"You said Angelina was in my bed. She wasn't there when I got there but I took your word for it and got rid of them. I wasn't about to keep them after that. I was thinking about you, maybe that's how you pulled me to you."

"I wanted you here pretty badly so… I'm just glad you are," I said and hugged him tightly. "I couldn't let Enoch see me like that, so I came inside as fast as I could. I'm sorry, it was the only way it would work."

"What are you… Oh. You want them to think we had a fight over this, and that I left," he realized. I nodded to him. "They'll leave, thinking we've ended our human\Devourer relationship and they'll both be back to chasing me across the country and the Horde will move on. That's actually not bad."

"I have my moments," I chimed and he smiled as he bent down to be closer to me.

"So, you didn't think I'd slept with Angelina, even with the evidence right there in front of you?"

"No," I snorted, "of course not. The Angelina ship has sailed."

"But how? How did you know the truth?" he asked softly.

"I trust you," I answered as if it was as easy as breathing. It was.

His hands rested on my lower back and he swallowed hard as he spoke.

"But how do you know I won't go back to my old ways," he said sadly. "I am a Devourer after all, and we are made to deceive and manipulate. I want it more than anything, but how can you trust me after everything I've done in my life, after everything you've seen from my kind the past few days."

"It's not about how you're like the Devourers, Eli…it's about how you're not."

"You are a magnificent creature," he murmured before kissing me gently. "Thank you, Clara."

"For what?" I asked dazed.

"For being level headed and not flying off the handle and taking the bait that Angelina fed you."

"You're welcome," I said and smirked, but it spread back into a frown. "Now comes the hard part."

"I have to actually leave," he said in understanding and nodded. "I wondered if you'd thought that part through. They'll see the string. They'll know if I'm still here."

It was my turn to nod.

"I know, and I don't like it at all, but I don't see any other way right now. You don't have to stay away long, just a few days."

"Yeah," he agreed. "And then what?"

"Come back here and finish school with me," I spouted causing him to smirk.

"I don't actually need to finish school, again."

"But you want to be with me," I said coyly.

"I do," he agreed and then chewed his lip. "It's for the best, for me to leave, to keep you safe."

"It'll work," I agreed.

"I won't go too far. I can't, and to be honest, I'm not sure it's such a good idea to leave you alone anyway."

"I'll be fine. You can make sure they're following you out of town first and when they are, you'll know I'm safe here. With the Horde gone, too, I'll be safe. I'll just wait for you to come back."

"You realize I can't come to physically see you before I leave. They'll be watching now, they'll know."

I nodded.

"This is goodbye, I know," I said softly

"You are so incredibly smart and lovable. You know that?"

"It doesn't hurt to be told," I said to him, but it was hitting me that he was leaving. Because of my stupid plan. Why did I open my mouth!

"Hey, you're right," he told me as he took my face in his hands, "this'll work. It's a genius plan that I'm sad to say I hadn't thought of. As long as the Horde stays away, we should be fine for a while once I come back." He let his lips touch mine softly. "I will miss you something fierce, CB."

"Me, too. It doesn't seem right; you leaving the day after I ultimately pick you out of every other guy in the world. You should feel pretty special," I quipped; my survival tactic. When things got tough, I got sarcastic.

"Don't I know it," he said gently and kissed the edge of my lips. "It's alright if you miss me, Clara."

"I will miss you."

"It's ok to say you will, and to be vulnerable with me."

"I'm going to miss you," I squeaked. "Please come back," I said against this chest. "Be careful and don't stay gone too long."

"I will do all of those things," he promised. "And of course I'll visit you in our Reveries. Until then, I hate to say it, but you're already late for school and if I don't leave soon, they may get suspicious."

I knew it was true, but I wasn't ready for him to go yet.

I pulled him down to kiss me. He was just as needy as I was, but I took as much as I gave. I pressed, he pressed. He groaned, I groaned. I dipped into him and gripped him for support, he did the same. It was torture in its truest sense. Way before I was ready, he pulled back and licked his bottom lip.

"Be cautious. Even though the Horde may not be waiting around the corner doesn't mean that it's safe for a girl to walk the streets at night."

"Ok. Wait- you're going to miss the Sweet Grass carnival," I whined. It was only two nights away.

"And the dance."

"I told you, I'm not going to that. But I did want to go to the carnival with you. Oh well," I said and put on a brave smile. "It's fine."

"I'm sorry," he said sincerely. "If I could be here by then I would, but-"

"I know. It's ok."

"I'll be back before you know it. And I'll see you tonight in the Reverie."

"Of course." I accepted his kiss once more. "Please be careful."

"That goes double for you."

"Deal."

"Deal. Bye, Clara."

"Bye."

And then he was gone. I was alone on my bed, late for school, and I felt as empty as I'd ever felt.

Eighteen

I trudged to school. Yes, trudged. I was late already so it didn't really matter. And if someone was watching me there was no way they'd miss the dejected look on my face. It was ridiculous, really. I'd never had someone consume my thoughts like this before. I looked at my wrist and the string was still there, as real and alive as it had been yesterday. Only now, it's stretched out to Eli who was no longer by my side but off somewhere without me.

I sighed, but stopped in my tracks. I thought I saw something white jump out of my vision into the bushes. I looked closer, but saw nothing now. I imagined Enoch, or Angelina even, following me to make sure Eli wasn't with me. I stood straighter and huffed my way across the street. I wasn't about to get caught in some word play with one of them.

I made it to second period just as it started. The rest of the morning was blurry and meaningless. I sat and tried to listen but ultimately didn't retain much of what was said. I made an effort not to look at people directly so they wouldn't question me about my eyes all day.

I did stop by Mrs. Gibbs' classroom and tell her I was quitting spirit squad. Of course, she'd heard all the gossip around school about everything that happened, but she was anything but sympathetic. She said she was disappointed in me for letting them drive me away from my dreams. I let her think what she wanted instead of trying to explain that it was never my dream to begin with.

Then lunch came. I made my way inside and got my tray of pizza and juice; a winning combination. As I squeezed through the kids to get to Patrick's table, I was stopped by a big body suddenly in front of me.

Tate.

"Clara, hey," he said casually, as if nothing had happened between us. He even smiled a little before it slid away. "What did you do to your eyes?"

"Contacts."

"Why? Your blue eyes were so gorgeous, why would you change it?" he asked with a hard edge, like he already knew the answer.

"They're my eyes. I think I can handle what color I want them to be."

He shuffled his feet for a few seconds and rolled his shoulders.

"I was wondering if you wanted to go to the dance with me?"

"No," I said and tried to go around him.

He grabbed my arm, forcing me to drop my entire tray onto the floor. I stared at him in disbelief, but he seemed just as stunned.

"Sorry, I didn't mean to grab you that hard. I just wanted to talk," he asked and looked around embarrassed as everyone stopped to see what the ruckus had been about.

"Are you still using?" I asked quietly. His silent, hard stare was my answer. I started to walk off again, leaving my tray behind as collateral damage, but he grabbed me once again.

"Stop walking away from me!"

And just when I realized that the entire lunchroom was going to watch him grab me and spill my food and not do a thing about it, an unlikely hero abounded.

"Let her go, man," Patrick said from behind me. I looked to see Patrick, Ike and that guy they called Buzzer all standing there. Buzzer was still chewing on his pizza. I turned back to Tate, not quite sure of what to make of the situation myself. He glanced them all over and decided they were no threat and went on.

"Go to the dance with me."

"No, I'm not going. If I was, I'd go with Eli."

"Why?"

"Because you're not my boyfriend anymore, Tate."

"You can't be serious, Clara. Ok." He raised his hands. "I get it, you made your point." He stepped a half step closer and whispered, but it was harsh and angry. "You wanted me to beg, to make you feel important and desirable? Ok fine, I'm begging. Now stop being stupid and come back to our table. You're just making a fool of yourself hanging out with these freaks."

I had thought I was helpless. I thought I needed Eli here, that he was my strength, my protector. But in that moment, I realized that though Eli was those things, I had learned something from him that I could now do on my own; stand up for myself.

"Screw you, Tate!"

I then walked into Patrick's congenial arm out for me and we walked back to his table with the buzz of laughter and 'Oh snap!'s and "Shot down!' around us. It hit me then how juvenile this place was and how I was so very ready to leave it behind.

"Wow, kitty," Ike said and made claws at me. "Raer!"

"Bite me," I laughed and took their good natured jabs gracefully.

The rest of lunch was spent cutting up and trying to munch down my new tray of pizza that Pat had gotten me in between questions about my eyes and where could they get contacts like that. The nose chain girl, whose name I learned was Ariel, was actually really cool. She worked at a clothing store in the mall and we both loved the same bands and foods. It wasn't everyday you found someone else who loved Ramen Noodles and fried egg sandwiches.

They were both something my mom had gotten me started on, her growing up in the south being the cause. She had been a Georgia Peach, through and through. Then she moved to Big Timber, Montana with my dad. They'd met at college and the rest was history.

"Ok, if you say your favorite book is by Jane Austen, I'm going to throw a fit," she said and looked really serious. I laughed and when I told her I didn't read in my spare time she gasped and looked like she wanted to slap me a little. I inched back. When I brought up my favorite vamp shows, she settled and was once again back on my side, though she argued that all those shows were based on books and that I should read them. I respectfully declined.

Math was brutal and long. Art was a disaster without Eli there to help me. When I eventually slinked into the house to find it once again busy and unruly, I rolled my eyes. It was beginning to be so hectic around there, I could disappear and they'd never know. I stopped and thought. Maybe that was a good thing, if impending doom found Eli and I in the aftermath of everything that happened.

"Can you watch the babies tonight, Clara?" Mrs. Ruth asked. "If I don't get out of this house, I'm going to go crazy."

"Sure," I answered, happy for a distraction.

They left and after a couple hours of building blocks and play dough, I put all the babies to bed. I then went to my room and got ready for bed myself, but it wasn't sleep I was ready for. I was nervous, I realized. I hadn't seen Eli all day and I was about to see him in the Reverie. I lay down and the second my eyes closed he was there. And we were in the sunshine in the park.

"Finally, Clara," he said and hugged me to him tightly. "I've been waiting for you."

"Sorry. I had to watch the babies for Pastor and Mrs. Ruth. I do it once a month."

"No, it's ok. I was just worried. And I missed you." He pulled back and then pulled me down on the grass next to him. I lay my head on his stomach and looked at him as he leaned back on his elbows. "Tell me all about school today."

So, I did. Even the Tate stuff as I said, "And so Patrick came up and was going to defend my honor, but it turns out, I could handle it myself."

"Tate is testing the limits of my patience," Eli growled, flopping back in the grass and running his hand through my hair. "I thought we only had to worry about the Horde and Angelina, but no, your idiotic ex has to rock the boat when I'm not there."

"I handled it."

"But don't you see? You shouldn't have to handle it. I should be there to protect you."

"But you can't always be and I need to learn to do things for myself. I've always let people do my deeds for me my whole life. It's liberating and exhilarating to tell someone to screw themselves," I said through a grin. "I feel all girl-power right now."

He laughed in an exasperated and indulgent way that told me he didn't like it, but was going to let me have it this once. I thanked him with a smile and ran my hand over his chest. I felt something. I lifted his shirt up to his chin. He started to back away, but I stopped him with a hand on his arm. It wasn't like I could physically stop him, but I was asking him to let me. He did with a heaved breath that meant a conversation was coming.

I saw the scar over his heart, the one I'd seen that day he gave me his shirt in the bathroom. I'd been curious about it ever since. I rolled to my stomach and ran a tentative finger over the large circular brand. The skin was raised and although it was healed it looked angry; like it once had been a very ugly wound.

"What's this from?"

"A parting gift from my parents," he muttered.

"What?" I asked horrified.

"I'll tell you," he said and nodded as if to talk himself into it.

"You don't have to," I said, but he spoke anyway, his voice haunted and shadowed with ghosts of his past.

"My parents were pretty angry at my lifestyle choices. After I left and ran away, they found out I wasn't forcing emotions to feed anymore. Angelina told them about a Sage, or a shaman priest, who performed exorcisms, but he performed them on those of us who are evil who may have been swayed or cursed by good." He laughed like it wasn't funny at all. "He called it Demoralizing. Funny right?" He shook his head and put his hand over mine over the scar on his heart. "They caught up to me, dragged me back to one of our homes in Amsterdam and chained me upright to an oak tree. Angelina, Enoch, Mara, my parents…they all just stood and watched as he burned and branded me over and over. We heal fast, so he'd wait for my skin to stop bleeding and then start again. It went on for days. Finally, he said there was nothing he could do, that I was a lost cause. My parents said that I shamed them and my mother actually spit on me. They left me there, chained to a tree in the valley of the mountains near our home, hanging by my wrist for five days. Then someone…found me. He got me down and I left, was able to evade them for a few years before they found me again, but not my parents. They gave up on me becoming the prodigal son."

"Eli, that's-" I sighed. "That's terrible. No one should have to go through something like that."

"It was a long time ago," he said and waved my fears away. "I'm over it."

"Really? I remember some guy telling me once that it was ok to be vulnerable with him. Well, I repeat that sentiment."

He let his smile cause me difficulty in breathing before pulling me up to lay on his chest. He stroked my hair, and inhaled long and deep before exhaling in a groan.

"You even smell good in my Reveries."

I let it go, he apparently wanted to change the subject. So I just said, "Eli, I just want you to know that they are the worst kind of scum for doing that to you. You and me, we're going to leave all this behind soon and you'll never have to think about it ever again."

"You're very set on leaving," he musing. "You won't miss it here? The Pastor and his family?"

"Of course, but I can't stay with them forever. The court agreement was only until I graduated high school anyway. And as far as this town? No, I won't miss it. The only good thing about being here was my parents and they aren't here anymore."

"Where do you want to go first?" he asked quietly.

"I've never been anywhere. Where do you want to take me first?"

"As long as I'm with you, it won't matter where we are," he answered and pulled my chin up as he seared me with a promising kiss.

Nineteen

"So who was the person who saved you?" I asked as he walked me back to my house. In the Reverie it was daylight, but we were all alone and the temperature was perfect. I marveled that I had the best dates with Eli, though we never actually went anywhere.

"Hmm?" he asked distractedly.

"You said someone saved you from the tree that day. Who was it?"

"Oh. No one. We'll save that part of the story for another night, ok?"

"Ok," I answered. "So…the carnival is tomorrow night." I produced a pout that would put Shirley Temple to shame. He laughed loudly and shook his head as he sat on my porch steps and pulled me into his lap.

"You're very good at that."

"At what?"

"Pouting," he said pointedly.

"Oh. Well, yeah."

"I would be here if I could. You know that."

"I know. I'll just go by my lonesome."

"No, you will not Miss Hopkins. You are on house arrest until I get back," he ordered sternly.

"Eli, I can't just sit at home. This is the last time I'll get to go. I'll go with the Pastor and his family."

"Oh, they go to the carnival too? That should be fine then. Just stay with them at all times."

"What are you so worried about? Didn't Enoch and Angelina follow you out of town?"

"Yeah, they did. I just don't want to take any chances. I don't want you alone."

"Is there something you're not telling me?"

"CB," he chided. "Don't worry so much, love." I gulped at that word and then took a deep breath. He slid his hand up my spine and back down again as I stared at him. "It's my job to worry."

"I thought I saw someone following me today," I said, but his hand stopped moving on my back and I regretted bringing it up. "Something…I don't know. It may be nothing, but I could've sworn I saw something white moving and following me in the bushes."

"Well, more reason to be extra careful. Please, Clara."

"Sure," I said and was a little confused at how he didn't flip out about it.

"I better go and let you sleep."

"Where are you?"

"I'm not going to say, just in case. But not too far. I couldn't go very far from you."

"Aha. Will I see you tomorrow night? When I get back from the carnival?"

"Yep, I'll be right here waiting . Be careful."

"I will. You, too."

He leaned down and kissed me, his fingers circling my wrist lovingly. His thumb rubbed my skin as his mouth moved and took mine deliciously. He then lifted me from his lap and with one final kiss to the top of my head, he turned to go.

He stopped to call over his shoulder.

"Have fun tomorrow night, why don't you?"

"I'll try," I shot back. "My boyfriend's out of town so it kind of sucks."

He smirked and waved as he said, "Bye, Clara Belle. See you soon."

"Bye."

Then I opened my eyes to the plaster ceiling above my bed. After a few minutes of sulking, I fell asleep.

~ ~ ~

The next school day was pretty much the same, minus the lunchroom Tate scene. I talked to the Pastor and he said they were going to the carnival and I was welcome to tag along. He was surprised I wasn't going with my friends. I said I was looking for a quiet night out.

On the way to the carnival as we walked, I could have sworn I saw that white thing again in the bushes as we passed. I looked closer but never saw anything and it would have been suspicious to go check, so I let it go. Reluctantly.

The Sweet Grass Carnival was in full swing when we arrived. The Ferris Wheel was the main attraction as always, with the line all the way back to the funnel cakes. I followed them around for a while before needing a break from the begging for more cotton candy. I went and got myself a diet soda and leaned against the side of the booth as I sipped it.

"Hey, Hopkins."

I turned to see Ariel and Patrick sidling up to me. It was dark by now and the pavement under our feet looked as black as dark water under the dim lights of the booths and rides.

"Hey! What are you guys doing?"

"Waiting for the Ferris Wheel to open up a little," Patrick explained. "They really should bring two. It's ridiculous."

"Yeah," I answered, "I know. I didn't get to ride at all last year."

"Well, come with us. Where's Eli?" he asked looking around for him.

"He's not here."

"Trouble in paradise?"

"Nah. He just had some things to do out of town," I said quietly and decided to change the subject. "So, does Mrs. May have a booth? I could chow down on some sweet potato fries right now."

"Yeah she does," Ariel said and looped her arm through mine, "and they're just as good as last year."

Patrick flanked my other side and we laughed at some mimes who were horribly impersonating a cheerleading squad. I guess that was the point. Then we passed Mike, Dee and Sarah. The dance must have been over already.

Mike was throwing rings onto glass milk bottle necks and cursing every time he missed one…which was every time. Dee and Sarah saw us and I knew an altercation was inevitable. I sipped my soda and looked away but that only made it worse.

"You have got to be kidding me," Dee yelled and slammed down her drink. "Really, Clara? You're taking this whole revenge thing a little too far I think."

"Excuse me?" I said, removing my arms from Pat and Ariel's and made my way to stand in front of her. "Revenge?"

"We all get it, ok? You want revenge for what happened so you're trying to embarrass us all by hanging out with freaks to diss us."

"And what exactly was it that happened, Deidre?"

"You and Tate. That doesn't have anything to do with the rest of us. We were your friends," she said, too softly and slowly for effect.

I laughed. Actually laughed. Patrick smirked in an ah-man-you're-gonna-piss-her-off-so-bad way. Ariel just watched with a curious expression.

"Are you joking or are you really that delusional?" She started to speak, but noticed my eyes then. She squinted and leaned in a little. "Contacts," I muttered to her.

"So now you changed your eyes color, too," she mused to herself. "Where's Eli?" she asked her voice sweet. "Did he get tired of you already?"

"He didn't want to run into you," I said and smirked to goad her. It worked as she then took to yelling instead of sweet talk.

"You're ruining your senior year! It's not like we're Juniors and you can just make it all better next year. You're tanking your reputation!"

"Are you for real right now?" My voice was shrill and confused.

"Of course I'm serious. Do you think your parents would be proud of you right now?" she asked and though all the breath left my body as if she punched me in the gut, I still saw her show coming into play. She twirled a lock of hair between her fingers and scratched the toe of her shoe on the pavement as Mike and Sarah stood behind her, watching as always. "All this; missing school, worrying the Pastor and his family with your erratic behavior, and this unfortunate business with poor Tate. He needed you, Clara. He's hurting right now and you just threw him away because he made a few mistakes. We're all just human, but that apparently isn't good enough for you."

I felt my eyes pop out, but I held it together. Mostly.

"After everything you did to me, you think I'm going to fall for that act?"

She looked back at Sarah and they shared a sympathetic glance at my expense. Then she looked back to me and said, "Deflection of responsibility is one of the steps of denial, I'm pretty sure."

"Yeah, but you skipped a few," I spouted back sarcastically. "Tate was my business and it was my decision how to handle it, not yours. Just because you screwed him behind my back doesn't mean that you had a say in our relationship."

Sarah's eyes went wide for a second. Mike just laughed. He loved conflict and goading, no matter where it was directed.

"Why don't you just go public with that, Clara!" she yelled and then took a small step forward, visibly calming. "Besides, it's your boyfriend's responsibility to be faithful to you. I didn't make him cheat, I was just the means. He used me, too, you know."

"And now you want my sympathy?"

"I miss you. We used to be friends."

"Before you slept with my boyfriend! No, scratch that. Way before that did you stop being my friend. I can't even remember when the last time you were actually my friend was. Probably in seventh grade, before you got your boobs." Patrick and Mike burst out laughing as Dee gasped and covered her chest in instinct. "But then you became a royal witch. You think you can do whatever you want to whoever you want and it's all ok just because you are who you are and your purpose is the only one that matters. That doesn't make you special, it makes you a terrorist."

She began to boil, I could see it, and the others had long since stopped laughing. I was hitting a nerve now, and I wasn't about to stop.

"And yes, it was Tate's responsibility to not cheat on me. But it was your responsibility to be my friend the way you say you are. And friends don't sleep with each other's boyfriends and friends don't pour chili on the heads of guys that our friends have secret crushes on."

Sarah's mouth opened, but she kept silent as she glanced at Patrick and flushed bright enough to see in the dark. I glanced at him to apologize bringing up the chili thing, but he was looking at Sarah with a little smile. Ok… moving on.

"You were never my friend. Stop being a pretender, Deidre. You're a nasty witch, just own it. Let's go," I told Pat and Ariel, who had stayed strangely silent the whole time.

Patrick waved to Sarah who pressed her lips to stop a smile and waved her fingers discreetly at him before turning to a fuming Dee. She marched towards us.

"You don't get to walk off like that! I haven't had my say yet!"

"I'm done with it."

"But Tate will be here soon. He was supposed to meet us. Don't you want to see him or are you too guilt ridden to see the hurt you put on his face?"

I turned, rolling my eyes, and as if fate was playing a lead role in the Broadway production that was the night so far, Tate was there already. He was standing against the spinning paint booth and he wasn't alone. Megan was grinding against him in a way that should be private and not seen with eyes that could sizzle into oblivion for it. He wasn't exactly fighting her off, given by the hands on her butt and the way his lips were giving her neck a massive hickey that would be impossible to cover up the next day.

Deidre saw at the same time I did and yelled at him.

"Tate!"

He jerked his attention towards us and pushed Megan off, who straightened up and tried to appear normal as she flounced towards Dee.

"Dee-" he started, but then saw me and he really did look guilty. It was ridiculous. He wanted me back, but couldn't stop making out with the school easies! "Clara," he sighed. "I didn't think I'd see you here."

I chuckled and glanced back at Dee. "Oh, yeah, he's really hurting. And he's all yours."

I looped my arms through Pat and Ariel's once again and kept walking amid their yells and fighting behind us.

"Good work, Hopkins," Patrick praised. "Nicely done."

"Yeah, seriously," Ariel agreed. "That was better than watching the Rocky Horror Picture Show."

I laughed, though I had no idea what she was talking about, and took another sip of my soda, but almost choked on it when I saw someone in front of us that I hadn't expected.

"Clara," Mara sang. I stared in silent disbelief. Eli's sister was still here? Why? "Hi, there."

"What are you still doing here?" I asked and came forward a little to stand in front of Pat and Ariel. It was weird how I had become some kind of protector for them. "Why aren't you with the tramp?" I sneered and she slapped the soda from my hand to the pavement. "Hey!"

"I suggest your friends run along and play unless you want them to join us." She gave a cursory glance to Ariel, but lingered on Pat. "Mm. He's pretty yummy."

I turned to them as I said, "Go ahead and get in line for the Ferris Wheel, why don't you? I'll be there in a minute."

"Are you ok here?" Pat asked.

"Yeah, just an old…friend. I'll be done in no time."

He nodded and they walked away as I turned back to her.

"Does Angelina know you're still here?"

"Stupid feeler. You have no idea how big this is. This is not about some age old squabble between my brother and Angelina. This is about this," she said and grabbed my wrist, but very gently. I saw our wrists were connected by the string. "You're bound to him and you sealed both of your fates."

"He left," I said steadily, proud of my composure. "He spent the night with Angelina. I told him to go away and he did."

"Wow. You really think we're stupid don't you? Surely Elijah can't be this stupid, too. He had to know the Horde didn't leave."

"They didn't?" I said and couldn't hide my fear any longer. The proof was when her lips opened and her tongue snaked out to lick them. "Why not?"

"Because they knew he was lying. And now here's the proof."

"You're going to turn us into the Horde?" I asked and racked my brain for a plan.

"I won't have to." She grabbed my sleeve and turned me to face the back of the building we were next to. There stood Hatch. "Not only are they here, but I'm one of them," she whispered into my ear from behind.

"You work for the Horde to kill your own kind. Charming," I said and let the sarcasm wash over me to keep away the shivers of fright.

"Clara, I presume," Hatch said.

Twenty

I had to do something, had to get them to believe me. I broke down and cried a little, which wasn't too hard given the circumstances.

"He cheated on me. I thought we had something, but I guess not," I croaked and peeked to see if he was buying it. I couldn't tell.

"We know he left town, this isn't about that." He crossed his arms. "Binding yourself to a demon," he mused and whistled. "Not too smart in my book. And he left you here, alone. So what does that say about him, huh? You thought you could wrangle an already tame demon, but even with all Eli's faults, he still couldn't be the human you wanted him to be, huh?"

"I don't care. I'm glad he's gone."

"Well, you see, you know about us. I warned him that humans who knew about us were to be executed."

I was beginning to wonder the same things he was. How could Eli leave if he knew the Horde didn't let humans go who knew about them? It had seemed strange last night in the Reverie, too, how Eli was so nonchalant about it when I said someone was following me. It confused me, but after everything we'd been through so far, I refused to give up faith in him.

He moved with a swiftness that I missed until it was too late. He jerked my arm in his grasp and Mara's arm snapped out in front of me. They stared at each other and she removed her arm and muttered a 'sorry' as she looked at the ground.

He started to pull me towards the woods at the end of the pavement. I jerked against him, but he tsked me.

"Uh, uh, uh." He pointed to the other end of the lot, to where Patrick and Ariel were standing. They were laughing and talking, completely oblivious as he threw popcorn at her that there was a Devourer behind them. I watched as Ariel's face changed from one of laughter to one of horror. She even grasped Patrick's collar as she looked around. He was confused, but held onto her.

Hatch looked back at me with a knowing look. He'd won and he knew it.

"Come with me quietly or Demarcus will torture her until she never comes back from it."

What could I do? I went with him.

I walked in between Mara and Hatch to a group of five Devourers about twenty feet into the woods. The grass was long, up to my thighs, and it scared me to walk in it in the dark. Although, with my new vision my sight was better, I still couldn't see my feet.

"So Mara was right. He did leave her here," one of them said.

"Yep. Let's take care of this quickly," Hatch answered.

But I wasn't going down without a fight. I turned to Mara.

"How can you betray your brother like this?" I asked loudly and they laughed even louder, except Mara who continued to stare at me as if I were disgusting.

"How do you think she got into the Horde?" one of the men said, but Hatch snapped at him.

"Be quiet!" He looked at me and cocked his head. "Mara, I wish you could do it. That would put the final stake in Eli, but I know the bond won't let you."

"I wish it were so, too," she spat out her words and looked at me. "Please get rid of her so I don't have this disgusting thing wrapped around my wrist anymore."

Hatch nodded and said to her, "We'll put your mark on her for you. Eli will know without a doubt that he is denounced and an abomination to our kind and better hope that we never find his traitorous hide again. Demarcus," he called to someone behind Mara. The one that had messed with Ariel was back so at least they were safe. "Hold Mara back."

Mara actually grinned and let him grab her arms from behind. I knew what was coming. They were restraining her so her instincts wouldn't kick in through the bond and she couldn't save me. One of the other men came forward without any further hesitation and yanked my hair to pull my neck back. I saw Mara jolt, but Demarcus held her tight. Before anything else could happen a flash of white caught my vision off to the side. I heard Hatch yell and curse before the Devourer let my head go. I stepped back, but we all stood still and watched as the grass around us moved in trails but there wasn't anything there to see. Another one of the Horde men yelled and went down into the grass. Then another. I waited for it to take me and grab me too. Whatever it was, was apparently strong enough or dangerous enough to take down a big Devourer.

When Hatch groaned I looked over at him and watched as he strained and fought against his legs. They buckled under him and he fell into the grass.

What in the....

I walked cautiously to Hatch and peeked at him through the fallen grass. He was completely still, eyes wide open...and they were black; completely, disturbingly, wholly black and bottomless. Then I heard a commotion off to the side but before I could see behind me, I was yanked down and dragged through the grass by my arm over my head.

I wanted to scream but for some reason, my vocal cords were frozen, in fear I guessed. It felt like I was dragged forever before it finally stopped abruptly. I lay in the grass, the sky above me. The stars and moon were shining through the canopy of the trees and in any other setting it would have been beautiful. And then a pair of beady eyes were above me too. I gasped and tried to scramble back, but it stopped me with a hand on my arm. It was surprisingly strong.

"Be still, feeler," it hissed in a high pitched and scratchy voice. "Those thieves will kill you if they find you. Be still and wait for the traitor if you know what's good for you."

I looked at it, or um, him. He was about as tall as my thigh with a white bohemian looking shirt on with his white pants and bare dirty feet. His eyes were beady and black. His hair was red and scraggily on the sides with none on the top at all and his skin had a greenish hue to the pale look of him. I had no idea what he was, so I asked him.

"What are you?" I whispered.

"Be quiet you stupid girl!" he hissed loudly through a mouth that was covered in blue goo. Devourer blood, I realized. His sharp little teeth were covered in blue, too. "What will it matter if you find out what I am if you are dead!"

"Sorry," I grumbled and that earned me a glare. At least I think it was a glare. His eyes were impossibly small.

So I lay silently and listened with a gangly miniature monster holding me down with his arm. I stiffened hearing the noises off in the distance, grunting and huffing. Then my heart stopped beating when I heard a voice I knew - Eli. And he was yelling.

I pushed the creature away and took off running. I heard him behind me, hissing and calling me names, but I kept running. I had told Eli that I wasn't into playing hero but apparently, for him, I was.

I arrived on the scene to see no one there but Mara and Eli. He had his arm wrapped around her neck from behind and there were several patches of grass around them that were depressed and indented so I knew there was a body there. I swallowed and focused on Eli, who had just now seen me. He first looked ecstatic at seeing me, then turned angry; the veins in his neck blue and raised.

"I told you to keep her away from this, Bengal!" he growled at me. I was confused, but looked beside me to see he was growling at the little person.

"She's stubborn and stupid," he said. "What did you expect me to do?"

"I expected you to do what we agreed upon."

"Never do deals with a Goblin. Didn't your mother every teach you that?" the little person sneered at Eli.

"Did your mother tell you to never cross a Devourer?" Eli rebutted.

"No, my mother said to bite first and ask questions later."

Eli sighed and gripped Mara tighter as she tried to twist away. I started to ask what was going on, but she elbowed him in the stomach and bent under his arm. She grabbed his head, bringing his face down to her knee. I started to scream, but the Goblin…Gnome…thing grabbed my hand jerking me to the ground and putting his scaly dry hand over my mouth.

"Stupid girl. Don't alert the humans with your high pitched screams."

I looked at him in disbelief and then back to Eli as he slammed her to the ground by a hand around her throat, but she didn't stay down long. She jumped up with a quick move back to her feet and then jabbed a blow to his neck with the back of her fist. I cringed, covering my face and turned away. I turned back just in time to see him as he grabbed her head from behind. He met my eyes from across the expanse and grimaced.

"Look away, Clara."

I obeyed with the quickness and through my squeezed shut eyes I still heard the crack of her neck and then the rustle of grass. I opened them to see him watching me, but he didn't move towards me. I wanted to run to him, but I felt vulnerable and strange. The way he was looking at me…I realized he was waiting to see my reaction to what he'd done; my reaction to the monster he thought he was.

So I ran to him. His face released all the tension, the blue veins on his neck and arms settled back into his skin and he opened the circle of his arms up to me. I collided with him and felt him lift my feet from the ground as he plunged his face into my neck and hair.

"I'm sorry," he said. "I'm so sorry you had to see that."

"You came back," I said breathlessly.

He pulled back to look at me and said, "I never really left. I just went far enough that the Horde would think I was gone and Angelina and Enoch would follow me."

"Really?"

"Of course, CB. I couldn't leave you."

"But you knew the Horde was still here?" I asked as he set me back to my feet.

"I figured. "

"But..." I was confused. "You left and knew they were still here...I don't understand..."

"You 're wondering why I would leave you in danger?" he asked with a little smile.

"A little," I said quietly.

"Well, that's where Bengal comes in." He turned me to the small man in front of us. "Bengal, this is Clara. Clara, this is Bengal. He's a Goblin who owed me a favor and has been shadowing you for two days."

"Um..." I turned to Eli so the Goblin guy wouldn't hear me. "No offense, Eli, but that guy's as tall as my knee. Why would you think he could protect me from-"

"Goblins have excellent hearing, human," Bengal said and crossed his thick arms in insult. "And how do you think I saved your bony backside the first time, hmm?"

Twenty one

"Um…" I scrambled for something to say, but Eli helped me out.

"Goblins are toxic to Devourers. Well, their bite is."

That explained the blue mouth and teeth. Eew. But it all fell into place.

"You bit Hatch," I said as realization hit me. "That's why he fell. You killed him?"

"I wish, but alas we are toxic not deadly to their kind. He's paralyzed. And he'll stay that way for all of eternity so he may as well be dead."

"Ok, that's enough for now," Eli insisted and pulled me to his side, his arm wrapped around my waist. "Bengal, once again, it's been a pleasure," he told him, but it sounded grated and forced.

"Bah, I hate you, traitor, as much as you hate me. We don't have to pretend."

"It's a strange partnership," Eli agreed, but reached into his pocket and pulled out a gold coin. He flicked it to the Goblin and he snapped his hand out to grab it. He grinned, his blue small sharp teeth blazing as he bit the coin, testing to make sure it was real, I assumed. Then he licked it and nodded, slipping it into his pocket.

"Business has commenced, traitor. The bodies will be taken to Resting Place by morning. My services are always open to you, for a price."

"Like I could forget that part," Eli answered. "Thank you for keeping her safe."

"Don't get soft on me!" Bengal spat and inched away backwards. "Business is business."

He continued to walk and watch us until he got to the edge of the clearing. Then he turned and ran. I looked up at Eli with a million questions in my mind.

"I know," he insisted and lifted his hands. "I know, there's so many things I need to tell you."

"The first one being, why did you concoct this whole plan and not tell me!" I said and pushed his chest a little to drive home my point. "Why couldn't I be in on it?"

"Because I wanted you to think you were completely safe. And you were," he said quickly, "I want you to understand that you were safe. I would never have left had I thought for a second that you would be in harm's way. But you gave me the idea. When you said I should leave and pretend to follow along with that for a while so Angelina and Enoch would back off, it was clear to me that the Horde hadn't left. See, the Horde took Angelina from the park that night remember? They don't take prisoners. Once you told me that she was still here, and free, I knew the Horde was onto us. I didn't want you to worry. I wanted you to feel safe. So I let you think that your plan was *the* plan. When in actuality, I called in reinforcements."

"Bengal," I answered as he pulled me through the grass towards the carnival. I noticed how he kept his arm around me the entire time as he steered me through the ones on the ground that I didn't want to think about. "How do you know him?"

"He's the one who found me chained to the tree. He's the one who saved me, for a price. I had to fulfill him a deed of his choosing. We've been…uneasy allies ever since. Goblins and Devourers have always been enemies."

"What did you mean their bite is toxic?" I asked and stopped him when he would have emerged from the woods. I had more questions still. "He said the bite paralyzes them?"

"Yes. They are paralyzed, aware and alive, but unable to move, and there's never been a cure. The Goblins have a place they take the bodies. They call it Resting Place. It should really be called Bragging Rights. That's all it is. There are hundreds of them all laid into the bowl of a valley. They go there and boast about how many they've taken down over the years. See, Devourers are Immoral, can't be killed at all. But, a Goblin's bite has been the only thing to ever take us down."

"And you brought him here, knowing he would follow me and bite whoever messed with me and that they would be paralyzed, unable to harm me," I worked out and he nodded.

"I knew they'd ambush you. So I made sure to come back and be here when they did."

"When did you come back?"

"This afternoon."

"Why didn't you come see me?"

"Because you needed to think I was gone for the plan to work. I needed them all together so that Bengal and I could take down the whole pack of them at once."

I sighed and put my hand on his chest. His heart beat against my palm and he was so close I could feel his breath on my face as I stared at his shirt front. It was black and plain to blend in with the dark. He'd planned this whole thing.

He lifted my face and ducked his at the same time to look at me. He smoothed the bunched skin between my eyes with his thumb.

"What are you thinking so hard about?" he whispered.

"I was so scared for you. One second I was so glad to see you and then the next I was horrified thinking that you'd get hurt or…worse. And then that Goblin dragged me off," I scoffed. "And insulted me."

He laughed and pulled to him as he said, "I'm glad you're still the same funny Clara that I left here two days ago."

"What have you been doing all afternoon?"

"Watching you." I peeked up at him to see what his smug tone was about. "I saw you take Dee down a few notches. I almost blew my cover to go and tell you how proud I was of you."

"You saw that?"

"Oh yeah, I saw that."

"And you were proud of me?" I whispered.

"Very," he whispered back. "I know you think that you are this weak, human, spoiled girl who has let people trample on her, but you are anything but that. That's the product of the life you've led, that's not who you are. Not anymore. You're capable of many things, standing up for yourself being one of them. I'm so glad I got to see you realize that for yourself."

"Thank you," was all I could say in response. "I missed you."

"Mmm, I missed you," he groaned and pulled me up on my toes to kiss him. He kissed me fiercely, but gently and when I felt his tongue ring against my tongue my restraint dropped from the picture. I pulled him tighter, causing him to groan which just fed my fire as he tasted my want for him. I don't even remember how long we stayed like that in the edge of the woods and kissed, but he suddenly jerked back and licked his lip. It seemed to be just out of habit because his face was serious.

"My sister," he said quickly.

"What?" I was confused why his sister came up in the middle of our necking session.

"My sister," he said harder. "Bengal didn't bite my sister."

He put his arms around me and shot us swiftly across the woods back to the spot we'd been before. He bent down and I didn't even have to look to know what had happened. She had awakened sometime while we were talking and sprinted away. He pounded his fist on the ground then looked back up to me and shook his head.

"I was careless. I was wrapped up in paying Bengal and making sure you were ok and forgot about her. She's long gone, back to the Horde headquarters I'm sure."

"They'll come back for us," I guessed.

"With a vengeance," he confirmed. "They'll know we ambushed them with a Goblin. They hate Goblins. This will be a worse betrayal than a bond to them."

"I'm sorry."

"No, I'm sorry. I should have be thorough. And I wasn't blaming you," he insisted and came to me. "They would have eventually heard of it anyway. I just hoped we'd have a little more time, that's all."

"What will they do? Just come back here and look for us?"

"I'm not sure. The Horde is in Amsterdam so we have some time. Don't fret about it. I'll figure something out."

"Why did she join? I know you don't view family like we do, but how could she do that to you?"

"It wasn't just me," he said thoughtfully. "In order to join the Horde you have to prove you're serious. The initiation ritual is to bring someone in to have tortured by the group, while you watch."

"Angelina?" I guessed in horror. "You think she brought in Angelina?"

"I think so. Only Enoch was on my tail this morning. That was another reason I came back today."

"You thought she was going to come at me, but instead she's... Wow."

"Ok, well there's nothing else we can do now, not tonight anyway. And you were pretty adamant about some carnival you wanted to go to..."

He smirked and held his hand out for me like a gentleman.

"You want to go play and celebrate after everything that happened tonight?" I asked him and heard my voice reaching for incredulous.

"You have to live for today, CB." He ran a finger across the length my jaw. "God forbid, there might not be a tomorrow."

"You're right," I said and put my hand in his. I sighed to calm myself. "You're right. Let's go." I looked at my clothes and was pretty clean for someone that had been dragged through the woods. The tall grass had helped I guess.

So, he walked me from the woods to the carnival. Once my feet hit pavement a calm settled over me. It was over, at least for right now. Eli was back and we were safe for the night.

We walked passed all the booths and a few rides before Pastor caught up with us.

"Clara. Eli, I thought you were out of town."

"I was. I surprised Clara by coming back early."

"Aw, how sweet," Mrs. Ruth chimed. "We're going to head back to the house. The kids have had enough."

"Ok, I'm going to stay, if that's ok," I said as I looked up at Eli. There was no way I was leaving him yet.

"Of course," Pastor said, "just be sure to be home before-"

"Midnight," we all chimed and then laughed.

"I guess I've said that a few times, huh?" Pastor said with a chuckle.

"A few, honey," Mrs. Ruth answered and started towards the house. "Come on then, let's go guys," she said to the kids.

"Have a good night you two," Pastor said over his shoulder. "And don't get into any trouble."

"We promise," I answered and muttered under my breath, "at least not anymore."

Eli chuckled as he pulled me to a hotdog stand, going on about how hungry he was. Which was impossible, Immortals didn't need food. He bought himself two chili dogs and I got a plain with just ketchup.

"I don't understand why you eat food if you don't have to," I mused and took a big bite as we sat at one of the picnic tables.

"Well, I started eating a few years ago when I began to go to schools. If I didn't eat at lunch people would get suspicious, so I ate for my cover. But I liked it. My first food ever was a cheeseburger. So now, I just eat because I want to. It's good."

"So you can scarf all the food you want and never gain any weight?" He shrugged and grinned right before taking a monster bite and then groaning loudly at how good it was. "Oh, bite me."

"It's not my fault," he said muffled through his bite. "I'm just lucky, I guess."

"Oh, you're lucky alright," I said and then laughed as he took my hands in his and took a big bite of my hotdog, too. "Jeez! You're such a pig!"

We laughed and wiped our faces before he asked me what I wanted to do next. I grinned. "The crazy house, of course."

"Of course."

As we stood in line I discreetly and quietly asked him the question buzzing annoyingly in my brain.

"So...Goblins." He nodded solemnly. "And witches and sorcerers." He nodded again. "What else?"

"There's many things out there, Clara. Sadly, I run into quite a few of them from time to time."

"But what about-"

"Can we just be normal high school sweethearts on our way up the bouncing stairs to the crazy house and not worry about that, just for tonight?"

"I think-" I laughed as I almost fell on the spinning wheel tunnel and he had to catch me. "I think I can do that."

"Good. Go! Go!" he yelled and laughed as the pendulums were swinging and he timed them for me.

Once we made it through the shaking ground, the room of mirrors and the quicksand bridge, we burst through laughing out the other side.

"We're alive!" I yelled.

"Where to next?"

"Thames!" We turned to see Patrick. They bumped fist, slapped hands… something. "I thought you were out of town, man?"

"I was, but I couldn't miss this. Where's everybody at?"

"Well, the guys had some World Of Warcraft convention tonight and Ariel was here, but I guess she wasn't feeling well so she went home."

"Huh."

"Well, you want to hang with us?" I asked though I really wanted Eli all to myself. But Patrick was alone.

"I'm gonna try to catch a ride on the Ferris Wheel. I've been waiting all night. Getting out of line probably doesn't help the cause though," he said and chuckled. "Wanna come?"

"Maybe later," I said. "There's something I want to do first."

"Alright, I'll save you a spot."

I nodded to him and then peeked around and saw one of those photo booths, the ones that draw your pictures instead of taking it to make it look like an artist drew you. I grinned at finding my prize. I remembered throwing away all my pictures of my life up until then, especially the ones of Tate. All the memories that I thought meant something, but were just a prelude to my real life; the one that mattered right now.

It was time to make some new memories.

I pulled Eli with me to it. There was no line so we climbed right in and Eli stuck some money in. It warmed up and counted down sixty seconds.

"I'm so glad you came here," I told him.

"Where else would I be?" he answered.

"No, I don't mean tonight. I mean…I'm glad you came to this town." I looked at our wrists, the barbed string still right there where it had been for days now. "You saved me from my life."

"Accept the things to which fate binds you, and love the people with whom fate brings you together, and do so with all your heart." I gaped at him and he smiled. "Marcus Aurelius said that, and he was right. I'm glad I came here, too. I would have never met you."

Although things weren't solved and we were far from done with this whole Horde thing, and lions and tigers and bears, oh my; I felt good. I knew things would be hard and dangerous in the days to come and I had no idea what to expect, but I knew if I was with Eli, we'd be ok.

"I feel like I…" I started, but stopped.

"What?"

"Nothing," I said. I was not going to tell him I loved him, not yet. I looked at the timer and smiled as I ran my hand up his arm to his neck. "It's almost time. Are you going to kiss me?"

As the timer beeped for us to be still and pose, his lips fell onto mine. We remained still until it beeped again, signaling us that we could leave. But we didn't.

In the booth, with a curtain covering us, Eli moved one of his hands to my cheek and one to my back to press me closer. He opened my mouth with his and ravished me in a tame and loving way that made me feel as safe as ever. And I let him. I let the emotions wash over me, so he'd feel the strength and truth behind them. I could tell when they were strong enough for him to pick up on. His grip tightened and he groaned the tiniest bit against my lips. I loved that I was the only thing he needed in the whole world, so I moved to sit sideways in his lap.

And I let him devour me once again.

The End For Now.....

Oh, the thank yous could go on for miles. First off, thank you to my God and my family. To the readers who have picked up this book and my others as well, you are the reason I do this. It's been SO much fun getting to know all different kinds of people from all over the world who have read something of mine. It's humbling in every sense of the word and I thank you for allowing me to be a little piece of your world. You guys are the best and I love to hear from you! You rock!

Be sure to look for the second book in the Devour series, Consume, due out May 2012.

Be sure to find and follow Shelly on these avenues for updates and information regarding upcoming books and sneak peeks.

www.facebook.com/shellycranefanpage
www.twitter.com/authshellycrane
www.shellycrane.blogspot.com

~ Playlist ~

The theme song for Devour is 'Not Alone' by Red

Song Title : Band Name

1. Time : Cute Is What We Aim For
2. A Daydream Away : All Time Low
3. Beautiful : Gary Jules
4. Lost in Paradise : Evanescence
5. Bright Young Thing : Albert Hammons Jr.
6. Sweet Dream Tonight : Tyler Ward
7. I Will Possess Your Heart : Death Cab For Cutie
8. All Night Doctors : Bush
9. Impossible : Band Of Skulls
10. Broken Drum : Beck
11. My Body : Young The Giant
12. Coming Up From Behind : Marcy Playground
13. Human : Civil Twilight
14. All The Same To Me : Anya Marina
15. Absolutely Zero : Jason Mraz
16. Kings and Queens : 30 Seconds To Mars
17. Sooner Or Later : Mat Kearney
18. The Lonely : Christina Perry
19. In My Veins : Andrew Belle
20. We're Ok : The Rescues
21. Monster : Paramore
22. Panic Switch : Silversun Pickups
23. Not Alone : Red

- A group of independent Young Adult authors who are dedicated to their craft -

Tiffany King, author of *The Saving Angels Trilogy*

Abbi Glines, author of *Breathe* and *Existence*

M. Leighton, author of the *Blood Like Poison Series* and *Madly*

Michelle Muto, author of *The Book of Lost Souls and Don't Fear the Reaper*

Fisher Amelie, author of *The Leaving Series* and *Callum & Harper*

Nichole Chase, author of *The Dark Betrayal Trilogy*

Laura A. H. Elliott, author of *13 on Halloween*

Amy Maurer Jones, author of the *Soul Quest Trilogy*

Wren Emerson, author of *I Wish*

Shelly Crane, author of the *Significance and Devoured Series*

Courtney Cole, author of *The Bloodstone Saga*

C.A. Kunz, mother and son author duo of *The Childe Series*

41765968R00164

Made in the USA
Lexington, KY
27 May 2015